THE CLOSER

THE CLOSER

A NOVEL BY

CAL RIPKEN, JR.

WITH KEVIN COWHERD

𝒟𝒾𝓈𝓃𝑒𝓎 • HYPERION

Los Angeles   New York

A special thanks, as always, to Stephanie Owens Lurie, associate publisher of Disney • Hyperion, for her invaluable guidance and sublime editing skills. She makes us look better than we are. Way better.
—K.C.

First Hardcover Edition, March 2016
First Paperback Edition, March 2017
1 3 5 7 9 10 8 6 4 2
FAC-025438-17020
Printed in the United States of America

This book is set in Abadi MT Condensed, Cambria/Monotype;
Octin Sports/Fontspring
Designed by Tyler Nevins

Library of Congress Control Number for the Hardcover Edition: 2015015135
ISBN 978-1-4847-2788-1

Visit www.DisneyBooks.com

SUSTAINABLE
FORESTRY
INITIATIVE

Certified Chain of Custody
Promoting Sustainable Forestry
www.sfiprogram.org
SFI-01054
The SFI label applies to the text stock

To the great Noreen Cowherd, the best mom ever
—Kevin Cowherd

THE
CLOSER

As soon as the pitch left his hand, Danny Connolly thought, Uh-oh.

The ball had come off his sweat-slicked fingers all wrong. Now it was floating gently to the plate, a weak waist-high fastball destined to be launched into orbit—possibly all the way to the International Space Station—by the glowering Red Sox batter.

Maybe the kid won't swing, Danny thought. Maybe he'll be so shocked at how lame the pitch is that he'll just burst out laughing.

But that was wishful thinking.

No, the boy's eyes were lighting up already, like it was a bacon-and-cheese-stuffed pizza sailing toward him. His hips were starting to turn. His shoulders were uncoiling. His bat was moving forward.

Danny winced. This was not going to be good.

What followed was a loud *PING!* that sounded like a coin dropped on a dinner plate. By the time he whipped his head around, the ball was arching over the left-field fence for a three-run homer, and the kid was doing a slow trot around the bases—slow enough to wave to his mother, his sisters and brothers, his grandparents, and every other person in the stands.

Bet he even waves to his dog, Danny thought, kicking at the dirt in disgust.

He looked at the scoreboard and sighed. Red Sox 4, Orioles 1. So much for following Coach's instructions.

"Just hold 'em this inning and we'll find a way to win," Coach had said, handing Danny the ball, clapping him on the back, and flashing a smile that was meant to be reassuring.

Danny stole a quick glance at the Orioles dugout. No, Coach wasn't smiling anymore. Instead, he looked as if someone had just rear-ended his car.

Even before the umpire fished another ball from his pocket, Sammy Noah, the Orioles shortstop, called time and jogged to the mound. He was followed by Ethan Novitsky, the rangy first baseman.

Neither of them looked happy.

"What . . . was *that*?" Sammy said.

Danny hung his head.

"I know, I know. . . ." he said. "My bad. Ugly pitch."

"*Seriously* ugly," Ethan said. "My little brother throws harder than that."

Danny managed a weak smile.

"Can you get your little brother on your phone?" Danny asked. "We may need him, the way this is going."

The two boys just stared at him.

"What?" Danny said. "Not the time for jokes?"

"Uh, probably not," Sammy said. "Instead of working on your lines, work on getting this next guy out, okay?"

He looked at Ethan and the two rolled their eyes before heading back to their positions.

As he bent down and grabbed the resin bag, it occurred to Danny that sometimes jokes were the only thing that kept his spirits up in games like this.

The truth was, he was having a crappy season so far as the Orioles backup pitcher. Oh, he knew what *backup* meant, of course. *Backup* meant not good enough to start. *Backup* meant we'll get you in there when we can, kid. Now zip it and grab some bench.

And with hard-throwing Zach "Zoom" Winslow on the team, a tall right-hander who could touch 80 mph on the radar gun, Danny knew the O's had a marquee starter who was one of the top pitchers in the league. Not to mention way better than Danny.

Which he could live with—at least for now.

The problem was, when he *did* get into games, Danny hadn't exactly been a shutdown reliever either.

That's what Danny wanted to be: the closer. When he went with his family to Camden Yards to watch the big-league Orioles play, he loved seeing the bullpen doors swing open in the ninth inning of a tight game and Zach Britton, their closer, come strutting out to the mound.

With the crowd on its feet and cheering madly, the closer would chomp furiously on his gum, glare at the batters, and blow them away one-two-three to preserve the win.

The closer came in to put out the fire—everyone knew that. But in his last five or six outings, Danny had been hit hard. And when he wasn't hit hard, he'd given up way too many walks.

He sure hadn't been putting out any fires. In fact, his teammates were starting to call him "Gas Can" Connolly for his habit of taking the mound and making the fire worse.

Great, Danny thought. A horrible new nickname to haunt me for the rest of the season.

Things were going so badly that, warming up in his backyard earlier in the afternoon, he'd even sailed a pitch over the bounce-back net and shattered a window in his next-door neighbor's house.

Cranky old Mr. Spinelli hadn't been home at the time, which was a lucky break. And Danny had slipped a note under the man's front door, taking responsibility for the accident. But he knew the gloomy geezer would go thermonuclear once he spotted all that broken glass.

Oh, well, he thought. I'll worry about that later.

He took a deep breath and tried to refocus on the Red Sox. Two outs. One more and at least they'd be out of the inning.

As the next batter dug in, Danny peered in for the sign from Mickey Labriogla, the O's catcher. Mickey put down three fingers: changeup.

Danny couldn't believe his eyes. A *changeup*? What was the plan here—to just *give* the game away?

To bore the other team to death?

Here he'd just thrown possibly the slowest pitch ever recorded in the history of youth baseball, and the batter had crushed it. And now his catcher was calling for *another* off-speed pitch? Another meatball that might end up in yet another galaxy far, far away?

Why don't we just throw underhand from now on?

Then he caught himself. Maybe Mickey knew something about the batter that Danny didn't. Maybe Mickey knew the kid was so geeked to swing for the fences that he might screw himself into the ground with some slow junk.

In any event, Danny wasn't about to shake off his catcher, who also happened to be the best catcher in the league and Coach's son. He nodded, took a deep breath, and went into his windup.

One changeup coming up.

PING!

This time the batter lashed a towering drive into the gap in right center. Danny's heart sank as he watched center fielder Corey Maduro and right fielder Katelyn Morris turn and race after it.

But at the last moment, it was Katelyn who ran it down, making a lunging over-the-shoulder catch before tumbling to the ground and raising her glove high to show she had the ball.

As the Orioles fans in the stands cheered wildly, Danny breathed a sigh of relief and headed for the dugout.

"Saved your butt—*again*," Katelyn hissed as the Orioles hustled off the field. "You totally owe me, nerd."

Good ol' Katelyn, Danny thought, shaking his head.

Encouraging as ever. Always ready to pick you up when you're feeling down.

Danny took a seat on the bench, and Mickey plopped down beside him. The big catcher's bushy red hair was plastered to his forehead with sweat. He grabbed a towel and began wiping his face.

"I wonder if I might make a suggestion," he began.

"If it's 'Why don't you give up pitching and take up the tuba,' I'm way ahead of you," Danny said dejectedly. "And I'm not even sure I could *lift* a tuba, let alone play it."

Mickey grinned and shook his head.

"No, my suggestion is this: next time I call for a changeup in that situation, you call time, okay? Then walk to the plate and smack me upside the head."

Danny looked up and saw that Mickey's eyes were twinkling. This was the great thing about the O's catcher: win or lose, he was always in a great mood. Which was why he was one of Danny's best friends.

No one loved the game more than Mickey did. And this, Danny knew, was Mickey's way of trying to make him feel better. The big guy was taking some of the blame for the near-disastrous consequences of that last pitch.

Danny couldn't help but grin, too.

"Deal," he said, and the two bumped fists.

"Good," Mickey said. "One more thing: you throw nothing but fastballs next inning, okay? No matter how many fat little fingers I put down. Just throw hard and don't worry about it."

But the sixth inning was almost as rocky for Danny as the previous one. He struggled with his control from the outset. He walked the first two batters before giving up a ground-rule double, the ball skipping over the fence and nearly hitting an old man in a straw hat and sunglasses who was watching from the shade of a tree.

A comebacker to the mound and a nice catch by first baseman Ethan Novitsky in foul territory kept the Red Sox runner at second base before Danny struck out the leadoff batter to end the inning. But the damage was done. And when the Orioles failed to rally in their half of the inning, Danny found himself feeling even worse.

Final score: Red Sox 6, Orioles 1.

It was their second loss in a row, and third in the last five games. As he listened to Coach's postgame remarks—it was the usual stuff about keeping their heads up and working hard and blah, blah, blah—Danny realized with a jolt that his lousy pitching had played a major role in all three of the team's losses.

The thought nearly made him sick to his stomach.

Mickey, Katelyn, and some of the others were going for ice cream, but Danny couldn't bring himself to join them and fake being in a good mood. Instead, he gathered up his gear, trudged out to the parking lot, and plunked himself down on the curb to wait for his mom.

At dusk, her SUV finally pulled in. When she rolled up next to him and powered down the window, he could see she was beaming.

Here it comes, he thought.

"Joey was awesome this afternoon!" his mom said.

Of course he was, Danny thought. Joey's *always* awesome.

"They beat the other team—the Titans, I think it was—five–nothing," she went on. "Your brother threw a three-hitter."

Hmm, Danny thought. Only a three-hitter? Must have the flu or something.

"The other team didn't have a prayer," his mom said. "Oh, Joey didn't have his best game. But he still struck out nine."

Danny cocked an eyebrow. Under double-digits in K's, too? Get that kid to the emergency room!

He threw his gear in the backseat and climbed in. Pulling on his seat belt, he counted down silently: three, two, one. As if on cue, his mom launched into a play-by-play of Joey's Metro League game as they pulled out onto the highway and headed home.

"Joey seemed a little nervous in the first inning, maybe because of all the scouts. . . ." she began.

This had become her routine since Joey's terrific junior season in high school had ended two months earlier, after he'd posted a glittering 8–0 record and college recruiters and pro scouts began appearing at his games.

Now that he was playing summer ball and lighting up the league for the Mid-Atlantic Marauders, his games often fell on the same night as Danny's. But both his mom and dad had been spending the bulk of their time at Joey's games, swept up in the excitement of their older son's exploits. And when Joey's games were over, it was usually his mom who was dispatched to pick up Danny.

On these nights, with her younger son trapped in the front seat beside her, she'd invariably launch into what Danny called "The All About Joey Hour."

"Your dad said there were at least four scouts there," she continued. "Plus there were two other guys with clipboards along the right-field fence. . . ."

Danny shook his head softly. *Clipboards?* They didn't even have iPads? What kind of loser organizations did they work for?

"Anyway, Joey's fastball was all over the place at first," his mom droned on. "But then he started to settle down. And by the second inning he was really locked in. . . ."

Danny stared straight ahead at the traffic on I-83. As usual, he quickly tuned his mom out. He'd been listening to this stuff for weeks and considered it a uniquely painful form of torture, given how badly he himself was pitching.

It was not until they were on York Road, only a few miles from home, that his mom glanced over and realized her younger son had yet to say a word.

"Oh, I'm so sorry, sweetie," she said, shaking her head. "Didn't even ask about your game. How awful of me! Tell me how the Orioles did."

Danny looked out the window. The truth was, he loved seeing how happy his mom was after Joey threw a good game, how proud she seemed. He never wanted to spoil these moments. After all, he was as proud and happy for his brother as anyone else.

"We lost to the Red Sox," he said finally. "But it's okay. Coach said we played well. He didn't kill anybody in his little talk after the game."

His mother nodded and smiled. "And how did my favorite Oriole do? Get to pitch?"

Danny stared out at the darkness again. What was the point of getting into all that now? Why tell her that her younger son—good ol' Gas Can himself—had come on in relief of Zoom and turned a smoldering trash-can fire into a towering inferno?

"I pitched a couple of innings," he said with a shrug. "Did okay, I guess."

Yes, it was a white lie. But he didn't want to watch his mom's face cloud over with concern, as it always did when she heard he hadn't pitched well. The way she looked at him—you'd think he'd just been diagnosed with a terminal illness.

She reached over and patted him on the arm.

"I'm sure you did just fine," she said. Then, after a pause: "Now, in the fourth inning, Joey had to face the middle of their batting order. . . ."

Danny sighed. Up ahead, he could see the streetlamps winking on as they turned into his neighborhood.

But "The All About Joey Hour" was still going strong. And as usual, there were no commercial interruptions.

Danny was lying across his bed, fingers dancing over the controller as he merrily wiped out the security robots of the evil Alistair Smythe, Spider-Man's archenemy.

After all, what was the point of being bitten by a genetically altered spider and given the awesome power of a million arachnids if you couldn't dish out payback to the bad guys?

Suddenly something hit his ear. He looked down to see a wet washcloth.

He turned to see his brother standing in the doorway smiling broadly. Joey was naked except for a towel wrapped around his waist.

"Mom! Dad! There's a sicko-pervert in my room!" Danny yelled, turning back to the video game. "Somebody call 911!"

Joey took a few steps and launched himself into the air with a loud "AAAIIEEEYAH!" He landed with a thud on Danny's back. The two went crashing to the floor as Joey laughed hysterically.

Quickly Joey pounced on his brother. He took hold of Danny's wrists, crossed Danny's arms, and pulled them back and around Danny's neck.

"Oh, he gets him in the Japanese Stranglehold!" Joey said, imitating the frenzied tone of a pro wrestling announcer. "The pain must be unbearable! Ladies and gentlemen, I don't see how this match can continue much longer!"

"Doesn't . . . hurt . . . at . . . all," Danny wheezed.

Then Joey put him in a headlock, squeezing around both ears.

"Now look!" he continued in announcer mode. "The wily veteran hits his opponent with the Brain Buster! Blood flow to the cerebral cortex stops in ten seconds! In twenty seconds, paralysis and even death can occur! For the love of God, somebody please stop the match!"

Somehow, with his face mashed into the carpet, Danny managed to croak, "Still . . . doesn't . . . hurt."

Only when Joey pulled him up by the hair, crooked an arm under his neck, and shouted, "No! Not the dreaded Sleeper Hold!" did Danny gasp, "Okay, okay . . . I . . . surrender!"

Joey shot to his feet and thrust his hands in the air. "Still the undisputed one-hundred-and-seventy-five-pound champion of the World Wrestling Federation!" he cried, dancing around the room. "The crowd is going wild! Listen to the chants of this sellout crowd: 'JO-EY! JO-EY!'"

"No, they're chanting 'WEIRD-O! WEIRD-O!'" Danny said, scowling and massaging his neck. "Why do I have to go through this every time you're a little bored?"

"Gotta work on my wrestling moves, bro," Joey said, flopping on the other bed. "And you're fresh meat."

He shot to his feet and flexed his biceps. Then, kissing each one lovingly, he pointed at Danny and shouted, "You can run, fool, but you can't hide!"

As usual, Danny couldn't help cracking up at his brother's antics.

This was how it always went. The truth was that Danny loved horsing around with Joey, even though these sessions generally ended with Danny being planted headfirst in the clothes hamper or tossed unceremoniously in the closet like an old duffel bag.

Despite the gap in their ages—Joey was a rising senior at Stevenson High while Danny was going into eighth grade at York Middle—the two brothers had always been close. Whenever he was home, Joey always made a point of stopping by Danny's room at the end of the day to talk or joke around, even if it was just for a minute or two.

"Heard you were All-World in Metro League again today," Danny said, retrieving the controller from the floor.

Joey shrugged. "I was okay. The Titans don't have too many sticks in that lineup. Don't let anybody tell you I was great, 'cause I wasn't."

"I don't know," Danny said. " 'The All About Joey Hour' had you mowing them down like Clayton Kershaw."

Joey grinned knowingly. "Mom gets a little carried away, doesn't she? Want some advice? Start wearing headphones on the ride home. Then you won't have to listen to that stuff."

That was another thing Danny admired about his brother: Joey never took himself too seriously. Even though everyone in town—including his two starstruck parents—seemed to be buzzing about the seemingly boundless future he had as a major league prospect, Joey didn't let it affect him. He was as modest and unassuming now as he had been two years ago, when he'd struggled as an inconsistent starter with an ugly delivery and big-time control problems on the Stevenson jayvee team.

"How 'bout you?" Joey said, sitting down again. "Did you light it up for the O's tonight?"

Danny snorted and shook his head.

"Not really," he said. "The truth is, I sucked. I mean, really, *really* sucked. If I was on a baseball card, that's what they'd put underneath my photo: 'Danny Connolly, right-hander. Five feet seven, one hundred and fifty pounds. Lifetime stats: Don't bother. He sucks.'"

Joey's eyes widened. "Whoa! What's going on here? Someone get hit hard tonight?"

"More like for the past three weeks," Danny said mournfully.

"Gotta stay positive, little bro," said Joey. "It's the only way to be in this—"

Danny cut him off. "You want positive? Okay, how's this: I *positively* suck. I don't know where my fastball's going. My curve is nonexistent. And every time I throw a changeup, they hit it so far you need a passport to retrieve it."

"Great line," Joey said. "Except you stole it from *SportsCenter*."

Danny nodded. "Guilty as charged. See? Not only don't I have a future in baseball—I don't have one as a sports anchor, either."

He turned back to the video game and pretended to concentrate. But he could feel Joey's eyes boring into the back of his head. And since Joey was being quiet, that meant he was thinking.

Danny knew exactly what he was thinking, too.

"Anything I can do to help?" Joey said finally.

Danny shook his head softly. Good ol' Joey. Always the first to look after his little brother; the first to worry about him when things went wrong.

Whenever Danny had a problem with any of the kids in the neighborhood, Joey would come to the rescue, defusing the situation before Danny started running his mouth and possibly got his butt beat.

It was the same at York Middle. Like when Danny had had an issue with Mr. Ferguson, his math teacher. Joey, who'd had Mr. F previously, made it a point to drop by the classroom after school. With his breezy manner and disarming smile, Joey had regaled Mr. F with stories about what a good kid and dedicated student Danny was— even though both brothers knew that last part wasn't exactly true. More like a load of bull, actually. But it had worked.

"Only way you could help," Danny said mournfully now, "would be to take the mound for me on Friday, when we play the Indians. Only I'm pretty sure the Indians would get suspicious when you tried squeezing into one of our uniforms. It'd be like Bruce Banner transforming into the Hulk. You'd be *shredding* those sleeves."

He looked at Joey with a sad smile. "And once you threw one of those ninety-mile-per-hour heaters that goes under the batter's chin? And the kid goes back to the dugout with his pants wet and his knees shaking, wailing for his mommy? They'd *totally* check your birth certificate then."

Joey laughed and held up a hand.

"Dude, I meant if you want me to check out your windup and delivery, see if anything's out of whack . . ."

"*Everything's* out of whack," Danny said. "Thanks for the offer, big bro. But I have to work out of this myself."

Joey shot him a sympathetic look. He climbed to his feet and headed for the door.

"Okay, let me leave you with one piece of advice," he said. "Ready? It goes like this: whatever you're doing now, do something different."

"That's deep," Danny said, rolling his eyes. "Very, very deep."

"Not really," Joey said. "Sometimes you just gotta change things up. If you normally warm up a certain way before a game, warm up a different way. If you usually throw a fastball on the first pitch, try a curve. Just do something—anything—to shake up your normal routine. Sometimes it helps get you back on track again."

When he was gone, Danny thought, How 'bout I never play this stupid game again? How 'bout if I throw my glove in the trash and torch my uniform on the front lawn in full view of the neighbors?

Would that qualify as shaking things up?

He could imagine the look on his parents' faces, especially his dad's, when he delivered that little bombshell. *Mom? Dad? Don't need a ride to the game Friday. Why? Oh, because I hate baseball. And I'm quitting the Orioles.*

If his dad was drinking coffee, he'd spit it halfway across the room. Jim Connolly loved baseball only slightly less than he loved breathing and double cheeseburgers. The idea of one of his sons not playing the game would be unthinkable.

It would upset his brother, too. Joey would try to fix this—Danny had no doubt about that. But Joey had enough on his mind already, trying to pitch well and impress the scouts every night while also trying to decide whether to sign a pro contract or go to college next year.

He sure didn't need his head-case little brother throwing a hissy fit just because he'd lost a few games, making things even more stressful around the house.

As Danny gazed around the room distractedly, his eyes came to rest on his dog, Scooter. The big chocolate Lab was curled up in a corner near the closet, doing what he seemed to do best: sleeping.

"What about you, Scooter?" Danny asked. "What do you think I should do about all this?"

At the sound of his name, the dog opened one eye before quickly closing it again. Within seconds, he was back asleep, breathing deeply and contentedly.

"That's it?" Danny said. "That's all you got?"

Apparently it was.

Danny sighed and hit the controller again. He was done thinking about baseball for one day.

Done thinking about anything except blasting Alistair Smythe's security robots.

Which were really starting to get on his nerves.

"You there! Boy!"

Danny had just pulled a stack of envelopes from the mailbox in front of his house when he heard the voice. It seemed to emanate from somewhere behind him, a thin rasp that hung ominously in the air.

He peered around and saw no one.

"Up here! My God, you're not the brightest bulb in the world, are you?"

Danny craned his neck skyward. Was someone in the trees? No. He turned and looked back at his house. He studied the rooftop and the upper-floor windows, then did the same with his neighbors' houses.

Nothing.

This was really weird.

Just then the flutter of a curtain from the house next door caught his eye. And then he saw him.

Peeping out of a third-floor window was Mr. Spinelli. His pale, wizened face was set in an angry mask.

"Stay there! I'll be right down!" he shouted. "Don't try to run away, either! Because I'll hunt you down! I'm a lot faster than I look. Once I get moving with this cane, boy, I'm like a cheetah, and that's no lie!"

Danny dutifully walked up to Mr. Spinelli's porch and waited. From inside, he could hear someone thumping laboriously down the stairs. Finally the door opened and the old man stepped out, pointing a bony finger at him.

Danny gasped and shrank back.

Mr. Spinelli's hands and arms were covered with blood. The white smock he wore tied around his neck was splattered, too.

I don't know if he can run like a cheetah, Danny thought. But it looks like he was attacked by one.

"What?" Mr. Spinelli asked, seeing Danny's horrified gaze. Then he looked down at his hands and chuckled as he wiped them on the smock. "*This?* It's just paint, boy. Cadmium red. Painting's my hobby. Got a studio on the second floor. I do mainly still lifes. Sometimes I even manage to get some paint on the canvas."

He broke into a harsh, wheezy laugh before glaring again at Danny.

"It's a very relaxing pastime—until one morning you walk into your studio and the window's shattered and there's glass all over the floor," he continued. "And you find an old baseball in your paint tray that looks like it was run over by a lawn mower and then chewed by a pack of starving wolves. *Boom!*—there goes your relaxation."

Danny felt his cheeks redden. He bowed his head and murmured, "Sorry. I left a note. . . ."

"Yes, I saw the note—misspellings and all," Mr. Spinelli said. "But sorry is not going to cut it, young man."

Suddenly he bent forward, his tall gangly frame making him look like a heron dipping to spear a fish. His face was inches from Danny's.

"Now let's get down to business, boy," the old man hissed. "Who's going to fix my window?"

"Me," Danny said.

"*You?* Ha! What do you know about replacing glass?"

"Well, my dad will fix it," Danny said.

"Your *dad*," Mr. Spinelli said. "And your dad is a professional in the glass repair business? With the proper certification? And many years of experience?"

"No, he's a documentary filmmaker," Danny said.

"Ah, well, that certainly qualifies him to—"

"But he can fix anything," Danny interrupted. "He's got, like, a million tools in the basement."

"I see," Mr. Spinelli said, rolling his eyes.

He reached into his back pocket and pulled out a piece of paper.

"But if you don't mind—and even if you do—I'd rather have a pro fix my window," he said, thrusting the paper at Danny. "This is an itemized bill for the damages. Give it to your father. If the man knows anything at all about home repairs, he'll realize I'm giving him a huge break on these prices. I'll expect a check within twenty-four hours."

He turned to go back inside, then paused.

"One more thing," he said. "You strike me as the sort of arrogant little know-it-all who doesn't take advice. But I'll give you some anyway. Baseball is a waste of time. I'm surprised your parents still let you play the silly game. You'd be far better off devoting yourself to mastering a musical instrument, getting involved in a school play, or joining the chess team."

With that he was gone, the screen door clanging noisily behind him.

Such a cheery old guy, Danny thought.

Walking back to his house, he considered what little he knew about Mr. Spinelli.

The old fellow had moved in about eight months ago, after the previous owners, the Millers, went to California. Tommy Miller had been Danny's best friend in the neighborhood, and both boys had been heartbroken when Mr. Miller decided to take a new job in Sacramento.

"I bet a new family moves in with a boy your age," Danny's mom had assured him.

Instead, within weeks, a rusty old Buick the size of a parade float had appeared in the driveway, and a skinny old man was occasionally sighted going in and out of the house.

"He must be very lonely," Danny's mother had said not long after Mr. Spinelli moved in. "He goes for walks every once in a while. But I've never seen anyone visit him. And he doesn't drive his car much. Seems like an awfully big house for someone who's elderly."

Would she be surprised to hear that the place had an art studio? For all they knew about their new neighbor, he could've put in a bowling alley and a drone command center, too.

Once back home, Danny tossed the stack of mail on the kitchen counter.

He picked through it idly and saw the usual assortment

of thick envelopes addressed to Joey. One was from the Atlanta Braves. Another was from the Boston Red Sox. Yet another was from the University of Maryland. The fourth was from Florida Southern, which Danny knew was a Division II baseball powerhouse.

Danny sighed. His eyes fell on the piece of paper Mr. Spinelli had given him.

There's the difference between me and Joey, he thought. He gets mail from big-time colleges and major league teams tripping over each other to land his golden arm. Me, I get a bill from our cranky old neighbor to replace a stupid window.

All because I can't even hit the bounce-back net in my own backyard.

One of us is doing something wrong, Danny thought.

And it sure isn't Joey.

Danny was sure he had misheard Coach.

After all, it had been loud at Eddie Murray Field when his mom dropped him off for the game, with a middle school band practicing not far from the Orioles dugout. It was even louder now as the band marched closer and launched into a spirited version of Carly Rae Jepsen's "Call Me Maybe," with the horn section blaring and the noise reverberating off the scoreboard and the outfield walls.

"I said, go warm up with Mickey," Coach repeated. "You're our starting pitcher."

"Me?" Danny said, dumbfounded.

He whirled around to make sure Coach wasn't speaking to someone else. But no one was there.

"Zoom's sick today," Coach said. "His mom called me an hour ago."

"He's . . . *sick*?" Danny managed to squeak.

Coach nodded and continued to fill out the lineup card.

"Oh, I don't know, Coach," Danny said, his heart hammering in his chest. "That Zoom, he's a pretty tough kid. I

bet he shows up anyway. I bet he gets here at the last minute all pumped up and ready to pitch his heart out."

"Doubtful," Coach said. "He's got a hundred-and-three-
degree fever."

Danny snorted. "Ha! A hundred and three? That's *nothing* for Zoom. That's like a day at the beach for the boy!
Now, when it gets to a hundred and five or six, sure, then
maybe he doesn't—"

"Plus he's been throwing up all day," Coach added.
"'Hurling' is how his mom put it. Torrents of nasty, pea-
green stuff. Sorry. Didn't mean to be so graphic. But that's
what she told me."

Danny nodded weakly.

I kind of feel like hurling myself, he thought.

He looked across the field where the Yankees were
warming up and groaned. The Yankees were only the best-
hitting team in the whole league, with three or four boys in
the middle of the batting order who looked old enough to
drive tractor-trailers for a living.

To go up against all that power when you've been getting shelled the past few weeks . . . the prospect made him
even more nauseous.

"You'll be fine," Coach said, as if reading his mind. "Just
try to keep the ball down."

Right. Keep the ball down.

Good advice.

Except . . . that was the whole problem. Everything
Danny threw these days was coming in flat and letter-high.
It was like serving it up on a tee to the batter. Like asking

him beforehand, *Hey, kid, where do you want the next pitch? Oh, up there? Sure, here you go. . . .*

But as he warmed up with Mickey on the sidelines, Danny was pleasantly surprised to see the ball actually going where he wanted it to go. This was somewhere around the knees, in the batter's Bermuda Triangle, where it entices a kid to swing, but prevents him from doing much more than hitting a weak grounder.

Hmm, maybe I won't suck today, Danny thought as he and Mickey returned to the dugout. He chuckled to himself. *Listen to me. Am I Mr. Confidence or what?*

When the game began and the first Yankees batter strode to the plate, Mickey and the infielders gathered around Danny.

"You got this, Danny," Sammy said.

"Totally," said Ethan. "You got this all the way."

Hunter Carlson, the third baseman, tapped Danny lightly on the chest and intoned, "You the man. Yankees are going *down.*"

Then, from right field, came another voice, this one piercing the crowd noise. "Just don't blow it, Gas Can!"

Mickey gazed balefully out at Katelyn. With her hands on her hips, she stared back.

"What, I can't say anything?" she yelled. "I'm not allowed to offer encouragement? I have to stay out here the whole time and keep my mouth zipped?"

"Unbelievable," murmured Mickey, shaking his head. "Always says the right thing, doesn't she?"

Danny shrugged. "It's okay. I'm good. Let's do this."

Once the game started, Danny discovered, with a sinking feeling, that his command wasn't as good as it had been in practice.

Breaking news, he thought. I'm leaving the ball up again. But he still managed to retire the Yankees in order on two ground balls to first that Ethan scooped up, and a hard line drive hit directly at center fielder Corey Maduro.

And after the Orioles took a 2–0 lead in the bottom of the inning on back-to-back doubles by Hunter and Katelyn and an RBI single by Sammy, Danny again held the Yankees hitless in the second inning on a pop foul and two harmless fly balls.

Walking off the mound, he permitted himself to hope again. *Could it be? Could I be finally coming out of this horrible slump?*

After all, he'd just gotten past the first six Yankees batters, no small feat. Their cleanup hitter was missing, for some reason, which was a huge relief. But as Coach had reminded the Orioles, the rest of the Yankees' "big, hairy-knuckled" hitters were definitely in the house.

In the dugout, Mickey plopped down on the bench beside him.

"Keep it up, D," he said. "Best you've thrown the ball in a long time."

Maybe, Danny thought. Or maybe he was just lucky. At times, it looked as if the Yankee batters were swinging with their eyes closed.

But all the good feelings ended in the third inning. As soon as he took the mound, Danny got himself into trouble.

He gave up back-to-back walks and a two-run double that tied the game at 2–2. Another walk and a bloop single in front of Katelyn made it 3–2 Yankees before he drilled the next batter in the thigh to load the bases.

"Here we go," he muttered as the kid limped down to first. "The Great Collapse is on."

Only then did Danny permit himself a quick peek at the on-deck circle. The sight shook him, as it always did.

Yes, there he was: Reuben Mendez, lazily swinging a big black bat, his shoulder muscles rippling through his navy jersey. Apparently he'd just arrived—the Orioles had seen a tan minivan scream into the parking lot, tires squealing, a few minutes earlier.

Great, Danny thought. Just what I need.

Reuben, the Yankees' star shortstop and cleanup hitter, was the biggest kid in the league. Coaches and parents of opposing teams wondered aloud how a kid who looked big enough to play linebacker for the Ravens could be playing baseball against their precious thirteen-year-old sons and daughters.

Which was why the Yankees coach had taken to bringing a copy of Reuben's birth certificate to every game. He'd pull it out, wave it in the air, and invite anyone to read it whenever the grumbling about his big slugger got too loud.

Adding to Reuben's mystique was his growing reputation as a mean, angry kid.

Every player in the league had heard stories of Reuben's antics: deliberately stepping on the foot of the opposing first baseman as he legged out a grounder; running out of the baseline to flatten opposing fielders as they circled under fly balls; tagging would-be base stealers extra hard in the face and neck when they slid into second—so hard it often left scratches and bruises.

The boy was a classic bully. Danny's dad called him a "sociopath." Coach called him a "loose cannon." Whatever he was called, there was no doubt that Reuben Mendez provoked fear in every team that faced him.

As he sauntered to the plate, Mickey called time and trotted out to the mound.

"As they say, this next batter needs no introduction. . . ." Mickey began.

Danny nodded. "I was hoping he was sick with whatever Zoom has. Parked over the toilet puking his brains out. But instead he's the picture of health. Plus he looks even bigger than he did three weeks ago."

"He blots out the sun," Mickey agreed. "Keep the ball down. Bad things happen if you leave it up against this guy. *Very* bad things."

Danny couldn't stop staring in at Reuben. "What do they *feed* him?"

"Whatever he wants, apparently," Mickey said. He smacked Danny in the chest with his mitt. "Okay, let's go. *Focus.* You can get him."

Sure, Danny thought. He watched Reuben take a couple of vicious practice swings. The bat seemed to whistle as it sliced through the air. The evening was cool, but Danny could feel himself starting to sweat.

As Reuben dug in, Danny saw Mickey put down one

finger for a fastball and place his mitt practically on the ground as a target. I know we want to keep the ball down, Danny thought, but that's ridiculous. That's like a target you'd give if the Pillsbury Doughboy was up.

But Danny did what he was told. He went into his windup and fired a pitch down near Reuben's ankles. It seemed to fool the Yankees slugger, who was so eager to show off his home-run swing that he flailed at it helplessly.

Strike one.

Danny breathed a sigh of relief. We're doing that again, he thought. He was happy to see that Mickey had the same idea. The catcher had his mitt on the ground again. Same pitch, same place, Mickey was saying.

Danny nodded, kicked, and delivered.

But this time Reuben wasn't fooled.

He reached down and, with a quick, compact swing, hit a screaming line drive that bounced once in the outfield grass before caroming off the fence in right center as Corey and Katelyn chased it.

By the time Corey ran the ball down and fired it back in, three runs had scored and Reuben was standing on third with a smirk and shouting, "That was too easy, pitcher! *Way* too easy!"

With that, the rest of the Yankees began pointing at Danny and chanting, "TOO EASY! TOO EASY!" as Reuben waved his arms like an orchestra conductor and grinned wildly.

Wonderful, Danny thought. "Too Easy"—another classic nickname trotted out just to torture him.

As if Gas Can weren't bad enough.

Just like that, the Yankees were on top, 6–2. He kicked dejectedly at the dirt and tried to regroup.

He wondered if anyone in the history of baseball had hit a ball harder than the one Reuben had just hit. That ball had been *crushed*. It had nearly smacked the arm of an old guy with a straw hat and shades who'd been leaning over the fence.

Wouldn't that be just my luck? Danny thought bitterly. To serve up a crappy pitch that sends somebody's grand-dad to the emergency room? But there was no time to think about that now.

As he waited for the umpire to throw him a new ball, Danny glanced into the stands and froze.

There, on the top row of the bleachers, was his mom, staring back at him with a worried expression. Danny hated that look. He'd seen it too often this season—well, at least the few times when she'd actually come to his games and seen him pitch.

What's she doing here? Danny thought. Doesn't Joey have a game tonight? Apparently not. Did this mean his dad might show up, too, when he got off work?

Fantastic, Danny thought. Just in time to see young Gas Can/Too Easy go up in flames again. Dad will be so proud.

But in the next moment, Coach called time and popped out of the dugout. He yelled, "Pitching change!" to the umpire and pointed at Sammy as he walked slowly to the mound.

Danny's night was over. He hung his head as he trudged to the dugout. Just as he hit the top step, he stole one more glance at his mom. She appeared to be dabbing her eyes with a tissue.

Oh my God! he thought. Is she actually crying?

What was that old movie his parents used to watch? The one where the crusty manager of the team growls that there's no crying in baseball?

"I'll have to have to remind her about that," Danny murmured to himself.

Only maybe not tonight.

Danny and his parents were at Joey's game the next night when his mom popped her big question.

"Why can't they have more positive-sounding team names in this league?" Patti Connolly asked.

Danny and his dad looked at her quizzically.

She pointed to the scoreboard that read: MID-ATLANTIC MARAUDERS 3, ROCKVILLE RENEGADES 0.

"Okay, so marauders are, like, raiders and plunderers, right?" she continued. "People who pillage and loot and rob. Like, you know, pirates. Not exactly role models."

Danny shot a glance at his dad, who gave him a look that said, *No, I don't know where this is going either.*

"And a renegade is someone who deserts or betrays a community," she said. "Like a traitor or a mutineer. Are those the kind of values you want your team to represent?"

Danny and his dad were speechless for a moment.

"So what are you saying, hon?" Jim Connolly asked, his eyes twinkling. "You wish Joey's team was called, I don't know, the Mid-Atlantic Merit Badge Earners?"

"And the other team was, like, the Rockville Recyclers or something?" Danny added.

The two of them cracked up and exchanged high fives. Danny's mom shook her head in mock exasperation.

"I don't know why I bother," she said. "Okay, fine, what stimulating topic do you guys want to discuss? The art of spitting sunflower seeds? The joys of scratching your butt in the outfield when the game gets boring?"

"Oooooh!" Danny's dad said, laughing even harder now. "Think we just got owned up, son!"

But Danny quickly tuned out the rest of the conversation and went back to studying his brother, as he'd been doing since the game started.

The truth was, Danny was looking for clues about how to get his own pitching back on track. And who better to provide them than Joey, the Metro League's premier pitcher this season?

As Joey finished the last of his warm-up pitches to start the third inning, Danny marveled at how poised and confident his brother seemed on the mound.

Efficient, too. There was absolutely no wasted motion in Joey's delivery. His windup was tight and compact, a slight half turn to his left, his glove held in front of his face so all the batter could see were his eyes.

His leg kick was streamlined, too.

It seemed like every kid pitcher around was imitating the high leg kick of major league hurlers like Max Scherzer of the Detroit Tigers and Johnny Cueto of the Kansas City Royals, flinging the front foot skyward like they were doing some kind of crazy rain dance or getting ready to stomp on an anthill.

But not Joey.

He had his own style, which could best be described as no-frills and relaxed. Yet he was still totally dominant.

Tonight's game was a perfect example. Here he was, throwing a one-hitter, effortlessly keeping the Renegades batters off-balance with a fastball that he moved in and out, and a nasty curve that seemed to break straight down at the knees.

He made it look so easy, barely seeming to work up a sweat on this sultry July evening.

Danny knew there was no point in trying to imitate Joey's delivery. No, Danny was too loose and awkward, all arms and legs coming at the batter, a pitcher who perennially looked as if he were about to fall off the mound.

He wasn't going to turn into Joey 2.0 no matter how hard he tried.

But he was hoping he could pick up a tip or two about tempo or mound presence or pitch selection that might end the nightmarish stretch of futility he seemed locked into.

Suddenly he was aware of a hand on his arm.

"Are you listening, buddy?" his dad said. "I said, let's talk about you for a moment. Heard you had a rough outing against the Yankees yesterday."

Danny shrugged. "Not much to talk about. I stunk—again. We lost to the Yankees, seven–three. Reuben Mendez hit a three-run triple off me on a pitch so low he could've used a nine-iron. End of story."

He turned back to the game. But he sensed his parents weren't about to let the subject drop—not just yet, anyway.

Right about now, he knew they were both looking at each other with tight, worried frowns.

"You seemed so sad when the other team was hitting off you," his mom said. "I wanted to run out on the field and give you a great big hug."

Ohhh-kay, Danny thought. *Well, thanks for restraining yourself, Mom.*

That's all he needed, a concerned Patti Connolly rushing out to the mound with her arms outstretched as his teammates snickered and the Yankees serenaded him with cries of "Awww, look who needs his mommy!"

"You're just going through a rough patch," his dad said. "But you'll figure it out. People struggle in sports all the time. You know that."

Danny nodded.

"Yeah, I do," he said. "Guess it's wearing me down a little. It's kind of been going on for a while. I never worried about being the best player on the team. I just never wanted to be the worst.

"And right now I'm kind of the hands-down favorite to win that award."

They watched in silence as Joey struck out the first Renegades batter on a curve ball that seemed to break from somewhere out by third base. It was so filthy the kid started bailing out of the batter's box before the ball was even halfway to the plate, then swung frantically when he realized it would catch the strike zone.

Joey handcuffed the next batter on a 3-and-2 fastball

that the kid hit off the bat handle for a weak tapper back to the mound and the second out.

As the next batter dug in, Jim Connolly said in a low voice, "You know, buddy, you don't have to play baseball if you don't want to."

Danny turned to look at his dad. Wow, he thought, the man was serious! File this one under *Words You Never Expected to Hear from Your Dad in a Gazillion Years.*

Mr. Baseball himself wouldn't stroke out if his younger son quit the game?

The man who'd been a gritty, good-field, good-hit second baseman for four years at Towson University before blowing out a knee—and yet was *still* elected team captain because he commanded so much respect?

The guy who'd been a season-ticket holder for Orioles games at Camden Yards since the place opened?

That guy was cool with his kid turning his back on baseball?

"I mean it," his dad continued. "Your mom and I have talked it over. I know I've only seen one or two of your games this season. But you don't seem to be having any fun out there. Which means you're putting way too much pressure on yourself. And that's not good for any kid."

His mom nodded and patted Danny's shoulder.

"Whatever you decide to do is fine with us," she said. "If you want to take a break from baseball, go ahead."

Oh, Danny had thought a lot about taking a break from the game, all right. He'd thought about it so much it made his head hurt and his stomach queasy.

But in the end, he knew one thing for certain: he wasn't

going to quit. No way. He loved baseball too much, had too many great memories about playing the game since he was six. Not only that, but he'd always loved being part of a team—even if some of those teammates were getting sick of seeing him suck in big games.

No, he was going to find a way out of this slump, even if it killed him. And the way things were going, that was a very real possibility.

"I'll be okay," he said. "We play the Tigers Monday. Coach said to come early and get a good warm-up, in case Zoom still can't go."

His mom smiled and kissed him on the forehead. His dad patted him on the back. Danny couldn't be sure, but he thought he spotted a look of relief on his dad's face.

"Okay, now that we've averted that crisis," his dad said, "there's another matter to discuss. I finally looked at the bill Old Man Spinelli gave us. What kind of a window did you break, anyway?

"You see what he's charging us? It would cost less to replace a window in the Sistine Chapel!"

"I'm sorry, Dad," Danny began. "I was throwing against the—"

But his dad cut him off with the wave of a hand.

"No worries, buddy," he said. "I broke plenty of windows playing ball when I was your age. But I'm not paying that ridiculous bill. Mr. Spinelli will just have to wait until I can get over there to fix it."

Just then, Joey struck out the third Renegades batter to end the inning. It was his sixth strikeout of the game. Danny watched as the scouts in their lawn chairs along the third-base line nodded approvingly and began scribbling in their notebooks and pecking on their laptops.

The great Joey Connolly, the kid with the golden arm, was wowing them again.

Joey himself celebrated in typical Joey fashion: with a quick, understated little fist pump as he jogged to the dugout.

Halfway there, he looked up in the bleachers at his parents and little brother and waved. Danny stole a quick glance at his mom and dad. Both were on their feet, beaming with pride as they clapped and cheered wildly.

One day, he thought, maybe I'll see that look in their eyes when I'm pitching, too.

If only that day would come soon.

When Danny arrived at York Fun Lanes, the place had all the calm of a three-ring circus.

Lime-green and cherry-red bowling balls were skidding down polished lanes lit up in purple and red. As the balls crashed loudly into gleaming white pins, bowlers cheered and high-fived each other.

Hip-hop music blared over the sound system. Flat-screen TVs flickered from every possible nook and cranny.

A clown wandered back and forth, blowing up balloons, twisting them into the shapes of animals, and handing them out to squealing little kids.

Old-school this place was not.

Danny knew it was the sort of modern "bowling experience" that would make his dad break out in facial twitches.

If a clown ever interrupted his dad's concentration as he got ready to let the ball fly, Jim Connolly would probably strangle him—right in front of all the kiddies. What a visual that would make on the six o'clock news, Danny thought.

Wandering inside, he spotted a banner hanging from

the ceiling over the last three lanes that read: HAPPY BIRTHDAY, KATELYN!

He sighed and looked longingly back at the main entrance. Why am I doing this? he thought for the umpteenth time. Slowly he shuffled over to where the rest of the Orioles had gathered around the excited birthday girl.

The fact was, Katelyn Morris was still a huge mystery to Danny. The only thing he knew for sure about her was that he couldn't figure her out at all.

She was definitely one of the Orioles' best players, a terrific outfielder and a solid number two hitter in the batting order. She was also a fiery presence in the dugout who kept everyone in the game with her nonstop cheerleading and her utter hatred of losing.

But she was also just plain . . . *weird.*

This had become painfully evident to Danny—again—in the moments immediately after the Orioles lost to the Yankees.

That was when Katelyn had marched up to him and bellowed, in front of everyone, "How come your brother's such a good pitcher and you suck?"

For a few seconds, she had stared at him, apparently waiting for him to admit that, yes, the athletic talent gene that Joey had inherited from his dad had somehow bypassed the youngest member of the Connolly family.

But before Danny could stammer out a reply, Katelyn had chirped, "Well, never mind. Hope you can come to my birthday party! It's next Saturday at three!"

Then she had turned and walked away.

The incident had left Danny stunned.

Who does that? he thought.

Who tells someone they suck, then invites them to go bowling and eat birthday cake and ice cream?

But here he was anyway, feeling like a dork for caving in when he'd promised himself all week he wouldn't go to her dumb party.

At the last minute, though, he had swallowed his anger (well, *some* of it), bought Katelyn a nice present, and shown up anyway.

But he sure wasn't about to walk around with a big smile plastered on his face, pretending he was having a great time with the girl who had embarrassed him in front of all his teammates.

Just then, Mickey walked up and draped an arm across his shoulder.

"I've got good news and bad news," the big catcher said.

Danny shook his head. "Why is it never just *good* news? Is there some kind of law against that? Some kind of law that says there always has to be bad news, too? Why can't anyone ever say, 'Hey, I have good news! And guess what? I have even *better* news, too'?"

Mickey listened to the rant and shrugged.

"I don't know," he said. "I haven't given it that much thought. Now, do you want to hear this or not?"

"Sure," Danny said. "Even if I say no, you're going to tell me anyway."

"The good news," Mickey said, "is they broke us into three teams and we get to bowl for an extra twenty minutes. The bad news—hate to be the one to tell you—is that you're on Katelyn's team."

Danny groaned. "Great. Now she can tell me how much I suck as a bowler, too."

"So bowl a three-hundred game and shut her up," Mickey said with a grin.

"Sure," Danny said. "And with my luck, she'll bowl *two* three-hundred games. Or I'll bowl a three hundred and she'll find a way to bowl a three hundred and ten."

"Pretty sure that's not possible, dude," Mickey said. "Don't think the scoring system allows it."

As Danny feared, Katelyn was as supercompetitive with bowling as she was with every other sport.

Sammy and Corey were the other two members of their team. And with the scores of all three teams automatically flashing overhead, it was easy to keep track of which was in the lead.

Halfway through the first game, the three male members of Katelyn's team were off to shaky starts. No one had yet rolled anything higher than a six, and, to make things even uglier, Danny and Corey had each thrown a gutter ball.

Team Katelyn was officially in last place, which did not sit well with the self-proclaimed captain.

"Huddle up!" the birthday girl barked, gazing up at the scoreboard.

The three boys looked at each other. *Huddle up?* What did she think this was, a Ravens game?

"We are not—I repeat *not*—losing to the rest of these nerds," Katelyn hissed. "Is that understood? You guys are absolutely *horrible*. Snap out of it! Now let's get out there and roll our guts out."

Roll our guts out?

That was a new one, Danny thought. How did she come up with this stuff? And was that even possible?

But the speech failed to have the desired effect. Sammy promptly threw his first gutter ball. Katelyn uttered a primal scream and buried her head in her hands, unable to watch anymore.

"She's making me so nervous, I can't concentrate," Sammy said in a low voice.

"Welcome to my world," Danny said. "Only now imagine you're pitching like crap. And she's getting all over you with that air-horn voice from right field."

Sammy shuddered involuntarily.

"You'll need therapy by the time you're fourteen," he said. "By age fifteen, you'll be on medication. You know that, right?"

In the second game, Team Katelyn mounted a mild comeback to finish second overall. But this hardly seemed to satisfy their leader, who spent the entire time shaking her head in disgust at the pitiful efforts of her teammates and grumbling about being stuck with a bunch of miserable losers.

"Is that fair? Huh?" she wailed to no one in particular. "On my freaking *birthday*? To have three of the lamest bowlers ever on my team?"

When they finished bowling, the party moved to a side room. As they waited for Katelyn's mom to light the candles on her cake, Danny felt a nudge in the ribs.

"Dude," Sammy whispered, "for what she said to you after the Yankees game? And the way she killed us with bowling just now? When she goes to blow out the candles, you should mash her face in the cake."

"Probably not a good idea," Mickey murmured. "The second she wipes the icing from her eyes, she'll kick his butt."

Ethan nodded. "She'll *destroy* him. Break every bone in his body. Then laugh hysterically while she drags his corpse through the building."

Quickly, he turned to Danny. "No offense, bro."

No, of course not, Danny thought. Why would he be offended?

Just because his teammates seemed unanimous in thinking he was such a geek that he'd get his butt whipped by a kid who stood two inches shorter and weighed ten pounds less than he did?

What was she, some kind of secret super-ninja?

Not that he wanted to find out.

When it came time to sing "Happy Birthday," Danny realized it was the first time he'd ever sung through clenched teeth.

Mercifully for Danny, the party was over a half hour later. He was almost out the door when someone tapped him on the shoulder. He turned and there was Katelyn, staring at him with a serious expression.

"Two things, and I'll make them quick. . . ." she began.

What now? Danny thought. Is she going to rip me for missing that spare late in the game?

"Number one, we really need a good closer if we're gonna win our league again," she said, jabbing a forefinger in his chest. "And *you* are the guy. Your arm's not bad, and you have okay control. But lately, your pitching's been *awful.* I mean, I've never seen anyone so bad. You have to do something to change that. And fast."

Suddenly she flashed a dazzling smile.

"And number two, you're a really crappy bowler, you know that? But thanks for coming to my party. It was nice having you here."

Danny watched again in stunned silence as she went back to help her mother gather up the presents.

He shook his head softly. There really was no one else on the planet like Katelyn Morris, he thought.

Not that she was wrong about his pitching. He definitely needed to do *something.*

For an instant he wondered what he sucked at more, baseball or bowling.

I bet Katelyn could tell me that in a heartbeat, he thought.

Somehow, he didn't feel like asking.

Five days later, against the Blue Jays, Danny
knew what he needed to do. He was ready to take his big
brother's advice.

Change things up, Joey had said. *Shake up your normal
routine. Whatever you're doing, do something different.*

Maybe Joey wasn't baseball's version of Dr. Phil. Maybe
he didn't have *all* the answers. But he sure knew way more
about pitching than Danny did. Joey was on the fast track
to the major leagues—even if he ended up spending a year
or two pitching for a top college program first. Why would
you *not* listen to someone like that?

So Danny had totally altered his pregame routine. This
time, before coming on in relief of Zoom, he had thrown
just five warm-up pitches on the sideline, instead of his
normal fifteen or twenty. He had pushed off from the right
side of the pitching rubber instead of the left. And instead
of using the catcher's mitt as a target all the way through
his delivery, he had looked up at the sky at the last minute
in his windup before briefly spotting the target and releas-
ing the ball.

Zoom had watched him get loose and nodded approvingly.

"Love the no-looking-at-the-target thing," he'd said. "The Blue Jays will think you're crazy. And having the batter think you're crazy is a definite plus for a pitcher."

Now, when the first Blue Jays batter strode to the plate in the fifth inning, Danny motioned for Mickey to join him on the mound.

"What would we normally start this kid off with?" Danny asked.

Mickey looked back at the batter.

"I don't know . . . fastball?" he said. "He's a skinny little dude. It's not like he's going yard on you. Why fool around with him?"

"Great," Danny said. "We'll throw him nothing but curve balls."

Mickey's grin vanished. "Nice to see how much my opinion is valued."

"It's not that," Danny said. "It's . . . no, it's too complicated to explain right now. Just go with me on this."

Mickey studied him for a moment and shrugged.

"Fine," he said. "You're the pitcher. I am but the lowly catcher, here to serve. Here to offer suggestions based on wisdom and experience. Only to see them shot down like so many doomed warplanes in battle."

"Wow, did you just come up with that?" Danny asked. "Pretty impressive."

As his catcher trudged back behind the plate, Danny nervously patted his right hand with the resin bag and glanced at the scoreboard. ORIOLES 6, BLUE JAYS 1. Your team gave you a nice lead, he told himself. The pressure's off. Now don't blow it.

Don't blow it. Wasn't that the delicate way Katelyn had put it last week?

He peered in at Mickey, who put down two fingers. Danny nodded. He went into his windup and fired.

It was a nasty curve, he could tell that right away. It had come off his fingers just right. And his wrist snap had ensured that the ball would break sharply downward, just the way he wanted.

Unfortunately, it ended up way outside.

Mickey lunged like a hockey goalie and backhanded the ball before it could sail to the backstop. The batter just stood there impassively.

Ball one.

Ball two, another breaking ball, was even farther outside. So were ball three and ball four.

As the skinny kid trotted down to first base, Mickey jogged to the mound.

"Well, that was interesting," he said. "You know, if we dug up home plate and moved it five feet to the right, a few of those would have been strikes. I'll ask the ump if he has a shovel."

"You're hilarious," Danny said. "But we're not changing our strategy."

"This is our *strategy*?" Mickey said. "To pitch so far outside they can't hit it with a canoe paddle?"

"I'll get it under control. Trust me," Danny said.

"Famous last words," Mickey muttered, turning away.

Danny walked the next batter on five pitches, all of them curve balls, only two anywhere near the plate. Now he found himself taking five miles per hour off each pitch to get it over the plate. The next Blue Jays batter timed one perfectly and promptly slammed a two-run double into the gap in left center.

As the kid slid into second base ahead of Corey's throw, Danny felt the familiar panic welling up in his chest.

The comfortable 6–1 Orioles lead was now 6–3.

Not so comfortable.

Somehow, Danny managed to escape further damage. But he owed it all to his teammates. The next Blue Jays batter hit a screaming line drive that Sammy backhanded while leaping high in the air. Corey caught another hard shot hit directly at him. And Justin made a nice play at second base on a hard two-hopper to his left, tossing it underhand to Ethan for the third out.

In the dugout, Danny was greeted with a glare from Katelyn and an uneasy silence from the rest of the Orioles.

When Mickey plopped down beside him, Danny whispered, "No more curve balls. We go back to mixing it up."

"Excellent idea," Mickey said. "Lose that crappy curve, dude. Fastballs and changeups only from now on."

But the change in strategy had little effect. After the Orioles went 1-2-3 in the top of the sixth, Danny took the mound and struggled again. He struck out the Jays free-swinging lead-off batter on a high fastball, then gave up back-to-back doubles that cut the Orioles lead to 6–4.

Hunter backhanded a line drive at third for the second

out, but the next Jays batter roped a single to right to narrow the Orioles' lead to a run. Then Danny watched in horror as the next batter launched a titanic shot to deep center field before Corey calmly reeled it in a few feet from the fence to end the game.

It took another full minute for Danny's heart to stop pounding.

Somehow the Orioles had hung on for a 6–5 win. But even as the rest of his teammates whooped and fist-bumped each other, he was in no mood to celebrate.

Yeah, we won, he thought. But it sure wasn't because of me. I was a train wreck—again.

I was Gas Can Connolly. I came in with a big lead and started another Dumpster fire. Without three or four great plays behind me, this would have been a disastrous loss. And after Zoom pitched his heart out for us, too.

One by one, his teammates drifted off with their parents or headed out to the parking lot to wait for a ride. But Danny didn't feel like walking or talking with anyone. He knew his mom wasn't due to pick him up for at least another twenty minutes—assuming Joey's game hadn't gone into extra innings.

He gathered up his bat and glove and slumped on the bottom row of bleachers, his head in his hands.

Then he heard it.

"Boy, you're a mess out there, you know that?" a voice said. "A *complete* mess."

Looking up, Danny saw an old man wearing a straw hat and sunglasses leaning against the backstop. He looked eerily familiar.

When he took off the shades and pushed back his hat, Danny's eyes widened.

It was Mr. Spinelli.

The old guy shook his head mournfully and sent a stream of spittle off to one side.

"Yes, sir," he said, "you sure need a lot of help."

The old man walked slowly toward Danny and sat down.

He wore a white T-shirt that said FEAR THE ARTISTE and plaid Bermuda shorts that were at least two sizes too big. On his feet was a pair of battered running shoes that looked as if they'd been used to chase weasels through a swamp.

It was a "look," all right, as Danny's mom would say.

"Been watching you stink it up for a couple weeks," Mr. Spinelli said. "Quite frankly, I don't know how much more I can take. You're hard on the eyes, son."

Danny furrowed his brow.

"But you *hate* baseball," he said. "And you still come to our games?"

The old man shook his head.

"Never said I hated baseball," he growled. "I said it was a waste of time. And a silly game. Both of which happen to be true. I challenge *anyone* to dispute that."

He thrust out his jaw and glared at Danny, as if expecting an immediate argument.

When Danny said nothing, Mr. Spinelli continued. "But by God, if you're going to play it, know what you're doing! Especially pitching! You have to pitch with a purpose, son. With confidence.

"But you—you're pitching scared. You're not pitching to win—you're pitching not to lose. Every pitch you throw screams 'Please, Mr. Batter, go easy on poor little old me.'"

Danny knew the old man was right. The thought made his stomach tighten again.

He'd been feeling bad enough right after the game, when his wildness and inconsistency had nearly killed the Orioles' play-off chances. Now, thanks to his grouchy octogenarian neighbor, he was feeling even worse.

On the other hand, he was also getting more than slightly irritated with this impromptu lecture.

What, Danny wondered, suddenly made Mr. Spinelli such an expert on the art of pitching?

What made an old guy who stood in front of an easel all day painting a stupid bowl of fruit—boy, didn't *that* sound exciting?—think he was Mr. Baseball in the first place?

Danny was about to ask this very question—as politely as possible, he'd decided. But when he looked over, Mr. Spinelli was staring down at his hands, seemingly lost in thought.

A moment later, the old man nodded and clapped, as if he'd arrived at some sort of decision.

"Okay," he said, rising to his feet. "Got a ball in that equipment bag of yours?"

Danny nodded.

"Good, let's have it. Then grab your glove and get behind the plate. Come on, come on! I don't have all day!"

Danny did as he was told. The old man shuffled out to the mound. A wistful look seemed to cross his face as he toed the pitching rubber. But when he glanced back at Danny, he waved impatiently.

"Don't just stand there! Get down in a crouch, boy! Like you're a catcher. Do I have to tell you everything?"

Like I'm a mind reader or something, Danny thought as he squatted. Like I'm supposed to know he's auditioning to be the oldest Babe Ruth League pitcher in history?

"Okay, get ready!" Mr. Spinelli yelled.

At once, a tremendous weariness came over Danny.

What was the point? he wondered. All he wanted to do was go home and eat and maybe blow away a couple dozen of Alistair Smythe's robot goons to make the world safer for Spider-Man and the forces of good.

Instead, he thought, I'm here playing catch with a crotchety senior citizen who's probably about to throw his arm out and rupture a disk in his back and end up in the emergency room.

He watched Mr. Spinelli rock lightly on the rubber with his bony legs and begin his windup.

The old man turned his hips and shoulders with surprising nimbleness and began to push off with his right foot.

He struggled to cock his arm—you could see he hadn't done this in many years and the move brought with it some pain.

Finally, he released the ball with a loud groan, as if the effort had exhausted every ounce of energy in his body.

Danny watched the ball float gently toward him, the seams rotating so slowly that the effect was mesmerizing.

Great, he thought. The old guy thinks he's doing me a favor by showing me a pitch a third grader could hit into the next area code.

Now Danny raised his glove as the ball wheezed the final few feet to the plate.

"C'mon, ball," he whispered. "Come to Danny. Maybe then we can end this lame exercise and go home."

The ball kept floating, floating, floating.

Suddenly it seemed to stop in midair.

Then it dropped straight down, like a bird shot out of the sky.

Now it was Danny's jaw that dropped.

He caught the ball and stared at it for several seconds. Then he looked out at Mr. Spinelli.

"What . . . was . . . *that*?" he managed to squeak.

The old man shrugged.

"I'm a little rusty," he said. "Haven't thrown one of those in years." He grunted. "Guess it wasn't too bad for an old codger, though."

Now Danny wondered if his eyes had played tricks on him. A ball couldn't just . . . *stop* like that, could it?

Like it had little air brakes?

And then drop like an egg rolling off a counter?

No, he thought. Impossible.

And yet . . . hadn't that very thing just *happened*?

He shook his head in disbelief and murmured, "Could you . . . throw that again?"

Out on the mound, Mr. Spinelli cupped one ear. "What? Speak up, boy! You're not in church, you know!"

"I said, could you throw it again?" Danny repeated. "Please?"

The old man huffed. "You got a lot of demands, you know that? Okay, once more and that's it! What do I look like, a pitching machine?"

But not only did he throw the pitch again—he threw it three more times after that, too.

Each ball floated in on an arc that would cross the plate at the height of a batter's shoulders.

And then dropped as if hitting an invisible wall.

When Mr. Spinelli walked off the mound, rubbing his shoulder, Danny stared at him bug-eyed. He was bursting with questions.

"What do you call that pitch?" he asked.

The old man seemed genuinely puzzled.

"Well, I . . . I don't call it *anything*," he said. "Haven't thrown it in nearly fifty years." His voice took on a melancholy tone. "There was a time when I could practically make the ball back up, too. Oh, the hitters *hated* me. Always accused me of cheating, doing something to the ball. Cutting it, putting pine tar or Vaseline on it to make it dip and dart. 'Doctoring' the ball, they called it."

He snorted and shook his head.

"But I never cheated," he went on. "Didn't have to. It was a perfectly legal pitch. Just because they couldn't hit it didn't mean there was some funny business going on with the ball. I resented the implication, I can tell you that. It got me in quite a few fights. I had a terrible temper back then."

As opposed to now? Danny thought. *When you're Mr. Laid-Back?*

Aloud he said, "So you used to play baseball? Even though you hated it?"

Mr. Spinelli's eyes narrowed.

"Young man, you insist on misquoting me," he said. "And it's starting to get on my nerves. Again, I never said I *hated* the game. If anything, I loved it too much at one point in my life. Only later did I realize what a frivolous exercise it was."

Danny couldn't stop thinking about what he had just witnessed.

Seeing a ball do what Mr. Spinelli made it do—it was like stumbling upon something you never knew existed, something exotic and mysterious and unknown to anyone else. Something you never thought was even possible.

And the more Danny thought about it, the more he knew there was another question he had to ask the old man.

The prospect was so intoxicating he wondered if he'd even be able to get the words out, or whether he'd start stammering and stuttering to the point where Mr. Spinelli would just get up and leave.

Danny took a deep breath and exhaled.

Okay, he thought, here goes.

Time to swing for the fences. . . .

"Could you show me how to throw that pitch?" he asked finally. "Please? I . . . I really need to know."

Mr. Spinelli turned to study him. His face registered no

surprise. It was almost as if he'd expected the question.

For a moment, he said nothing. Danny's heart began to sink.

"Okay," the old man said finally, "but I'm only gonna show you *once.* It's not like I have all day to help every crappy kid pitcher in the whole country."

"No, sir," Danny said quickly. "Of course you don't. I'm sure you're a busy man. But if you could just help this one crappy pitcher, that crappy pitcher would be supergrateful."

For an instant, Mr. Spinelli's mouth seemed to twitch, almost as if a smile were about to form.

But it didn't.

"Okay," he barked. "Watch and learn."

He gripped the ball with four fingers along the top seam and his thumb positioned in the middle underneath.

"You want the batter to think it's like any other pitch coming," he explained. "So you keep your windup and delivery the same. But when you release the ball, you snap your wrist like . . . *this.*"

He moved his hand and arm slowly so Danny could see what the downward motion looked like.

"Okay, you try it," he said. He flipped Danny the ball and scooped up his glove. Then he walked back to the plate and crouched down.

As he stood on the mound, Danny was suddenly nervous.

He felt the way he did before a big test in school, or a tryout for a new sports team. Only if he screwed up now, instead of having to face the disappointment of a teacher or coach, he'd have to deal with a grumpy senior citizen who probably just wanted to get home in time to watch a World War II documentary before going to bed.

Danny gripped the ball the way he'd been shown, rocked, and fired, snapping his wrist hard.

The pitch floated to the plate.

For an instant, he could imagine a hitter standing there, bat held high, licking his lips in anticipation of launching this tantalizing piece of junk into space.

Then the most wondrous thing happened.

The ball dropped out of the sky and dove for the plate, where Mr. Spinelli's glove was waiting.

It landed with a soft *thwump*.

Danny let out a whoop, then punched the air with his fist, which drew an annoyed look from Mr. Spinelli.

"Don't go thinking you're anything special!" he barked. "I could teach a chimpanzee to throw this pitch if I had to. The key now is to keep practicing, until you can throw it without even thinking."

But Danny wasn't listening. He was so happy, he was on autopilot.

He ran toward the old man with his arms outstretched, ready to give him the biggest hug he'd ever given anyone.

But Mr. Spinelli quickly waved him off.

"Yeah, yeah, you're welcome," he said irritably. "Can I go home now? It's about two hours after my regular dinnertime."

Just then Danny heard a car horn. He turned and saw his mother waving from the parking lot.

"One more thing," Mr. Spinelli said as he turned to leave.

"Tell your dad he did an okay job fixing my studio window. Strictly okay. But tell him if he had any brains, he wouldn't let his kid play ball and go around busting windows in the first place."

Danny grinned and waved at the retreating figure.

No, he thought happily, I don't think I'll pass that one along to Dad.

Especially not now.

Mickey swept a finger across his tablet and the blue-white screen glowed to life.

"What was the old guy's name again?" he asked.

"Spinelli," Danny said. "Anthony Giuseppe Spinelli. At least that's what it said on a letter for him that was accidentally left at our house."

Mickey tapped silently for a moment, then grunted.

"Okay," he said finally, "this *has* to be him. He said he played a little ball back in the day? He wasn't kidding. Check this out."

It was the next morning, and the two boys were in the basement at Mickey's house, attempting a little cyber-detective work.

Danny had been so excited about learning his new pitch that he'd barely slept the night before. Right after breakfast he had called Mickey and begged him to meet him at a nearby park with his mitt.

For ten minutes Danny had thrown to the big catcher,

the ball braking and dipping even more dramatically than it had the day before.

When the demonstration was over, Mickey had grinned, given him the thumbs-up sign, and said, "Dude, looks like you got yourself one sick new pitch."

Now they were gazing at Mickey's iPad and an old story from *The Baltimore Sun*.

LOCAL MAN HAS NO REGRETS ABOUT SPURNING PROMISING BASEBALL CAREER

As a handsome star pitcher on the University of Maryland's baseball team in the 1960s, Tony Spinelli appeared to have it made. Aided by a so-called eephus pitch—a low-speed junk ball that opposing batters found almost impossible to hit—Spinelli won 12 games and was heavily scouted by a number of major league teams, among them the Baltimore Orioles, New York Yankees, and Los Angeles Dodgers.

"Eephus?" Danny said. "That's so lame. That might be the lamest name I've ever heard for a pitch."

"Yeah," Mickey agreed. "We gotta work on a new name. Eephus sounds like something you'd call your dog. Or maybe not even your dog—your parrot."

They read on.

But Spinelli shocked the Terrapin coaches and his team-mates by abruptly quitting the team after his sophomore season, just days after striking out 11 of the first 12 batters he faced in a 4–0 win over Clemson University in the Atlantic Coast Conference championship game.

"I'll be seeing that 'junk' pitch in my nightmares," Tigers cleanup hitter Marty O'Reilly told the Clemson student newspaper of Spinelli's performance.

The lone Tiger to get a hit, first baseman Cleon Massey, later admitted to having been so frustrated that he closed his eyes and simply threw the bat where he thought one of the junk pitches would drop.

"Somehow it made contact," Massey said with a laugh, "and I was lucky enough to leg out a slow roller down the third-base line. Make sure you emphasize the word 'lucky.'"

Spinelli went on to have a long and successful career as an architect. But the mystery of why he walked away from the game at the peak of his success lives on.

Interviewed by the *Sun* in 2000, on the 40th anniversary of his pitching gem in the ACC title game, Spinelli declined to elaborate on why he quit baseball.

"Let's just say one minute I loved it, the next minute I didn't," he said. "And we'll leave it at that."

When they finished reading, the two boys looked at each other.

"Wow," Mickey said. "What a story! And how cool is it that he was willing to show you his secret pitch? He just came up to you out of nowhere, right?"

"I think he felt sorry for me," Danny said. "Guess he

doesn't have much to do, so he goes down to the field a few nights a week to watch our games." He laughed ruefully. "Imagine going to a game to relax and having to watch me get drilled night after night. No wonder he had to help me. Probably couldn't take seeing that anymore."

Mickey grinned. "How do you think I felt? *I'm* the one who had a close-up view of you getting pounded. You owe me big-time, dude. A large snowball after every game for, oh, the next ten years ought to make up for it."

Danny jabbed him playfully in his ample gut. "Yeah, that's just what you need, more sugary, calorie-laden treats. With marshmallow toppings, too!"

"Oh, that's harsh," Mickey said. "My weight hasn't affected my lightning reflexes and catlike quickness, though."

Danny couldn't argue with that.

As big as Mickey was, he was surprisingly nimble. No other catcher in the league moved side to side on his knees and blocked pitches as well as Mickey. That was the main reason Danny wasn't worried about his new pitch handcuffing the big guy.

Mickey would be able to handle it. Watching him scoop pitches out of the dirt was like watching an artist at work. He could just as easily pluck this new pitch out of the air, Danny was sure.

"Have you told anyone else about this?" Mickey asked.

"Not yet," Danny said. "Not even Joey. And you can't tell anyone either, okay? Especially your dad."

Mickey smiled. "Uh-oh, do I have to do something weird? Like swear on a Bible?"

"Nah," Danny said, "we'll just prick your finger and make you take a blood oath. Something along the lines of 'I'd rather burn in hell than reveal the existence of my good friend Danny's secret pitch.'"

Joking aside, Danny was serious about wanting to keep the new pitch under wraps for a few days, until he could debut it when the Orioles played the Rays.

He couldn't wait for the reaction of his teammates—especially bigmouth "you suck but please come to my party" Katelyn—when he threw it in a real game and tied the other team's hitters in knots.

It would be awesome to surprise Coach, too—good old Coach, who had stuck with him and kept using him in relief, even when some of his teammates were calling him Gas Can Connolly and making it clear their four-year-old brother could do a better job.

Mostly, though, Danny wanted to see the looks on his parents' faces when he mowed down the Rays lineup for the first time.

He wanted to see them beam with pride like they did at Joey's games. And after looking up the Marauders' schedule, Danny knew Joey didn't have a game Friday night, which just about ensured that both his mom and dad would be in the stands.

Maybe Joey would even make an appearance! Danny thought.

Thinking about his older brother, he felt a stab of guilt.

Lately the gushing about Joey had reached epic proportions in the Connolly household. And Danny knew he hadn't been handling it well.

The other day, his mom had come up to his room and gone on and on about how great Joey had thrown in batting practice.

Danny had managed to listen to her for a full two minutes before erupting.

"Seriously, Mom?" he had barked. "Now I have to hear how good Joey looks at *practice*?"

His mom had frowned and said, "Well, aren't you Mr. Grumpy today? I would think you'd be happy to hear about your brother's exploits."

"Exploits?" Danny had snapped. "It was just *practice.* There are no *exploits* in practice. Practice is where you work on your hitting and fielding and pitching for maybe fifteen minutes. Then you stand around and look bored for another hour while everyone else on the team works on *their* hitting and fielding and pitching."

For a moment he'd been tempted to launch into the infamous rant of former Philadelphia 76ers guard Allen Iverson, the one Danny's dad had showed him on YouTube because he'd found it so hilarious.

Iverson had screamed to the Philly media, "Listen, we're talking about practice. *Practice!* Not a game! Not a game! I mean, how silly is that? We're talking about *practice!*"

But before Danny could, his mom had turned on her heel and stomped out of the room.

Recalling the conversation now, he regretted snapping at her.

She was right: he *had* been Mr. Grumpy. Or Mr. Major Mood Disorder—that might have been closer to the truth.

But maybe he wouldn't be after the next Orioles game.

Maybe all that would change now that he was throwing the coolest pitch he'd ever seen, one that could make batters look ridiculous.

Danny couldn't wait to find out.

The ride to the field for the Rays game seemed to take forever.

Danny couldn't remember his mom ever driving so slowly before. Did she *really* have to stop at each and every stop sign for five seconds?

Did she *really* have to look fifteen different ways at each intersection before making a turn?

Not that these moves were terribly unusual. The fact was, Joey and Danny had made fun of their mom's driving for years. They kidded that she drove like a nun—Sister Patti, they called her—and they warned her not to whack them with her rosary beads or they'd tell the mother superior and get her in trouble.

But today Danny wasn't laughing about his mom's turtle pace behind the wheel.

Today it was driving him nuts.

Finally he couldn't take it anymore. "C'mon, Mom," he implored. "Punch it!"

She looked over at him and sighed.

"Can't punch it here, hon," she said. "Speed limit's forty-five. And there are police cars everywhere. Haven't we gone over this a thousand times? You want to see your dear old mom go to the slammer? Then who's going to cook for you people? God knows none of you can cook for yourselves."

Danny snorted. This was an old routine of hers. *They'll take poor little ol' me to jail, and then you'll be sorry. What will you kids do by yourselves when you can't even open a can of soup?*

But he wasn't buying it today.

"Yeah, right," he said. "Worst that'll happen is you get a speeding ticket. Big deal."

"Oh, so it's not a big deal?" his mom said. "You want to pay my car insurance when the rate skyrockets, smart guy? All due to a ticket I got for driving like a crazy person because my son—for some ungodly reason—had to get to his game way earlier than the rest of the kids?"

She looked at him again. "And why *are* you so antsy anyway? You've been like this since you woke up."

Danny shrugged and went back to staring out the window, groaning silently over the endless drive.

Yeah, he was *antsy*, whatever that meant.

The good news was that his mom at least would be at the game to watch him. The bad news was that his dad was working late. And Joey had gone to the movies with his girlfriend to see some dumb *Planet of the Apes* sequel.

Initially, Danny was bummed that neither would be in the stands. But he knew that his mom would fill them in about his outing soon enough. Heck, sometimes Patti Connolly's postgame play-by-play recap was better than actually being there live. Her breathless tone and dramatic flourishes could make even a routine performance by one of her sons sound like it came in the nick of time, during the ninth inning of the seventh game of the World Series, with two outs and the bases loaded.

When they finally got to the field, Danny made a beeline for Mickey.

"If it isn't Mr. Eephus himself," Mickey said.

"Shhhh, not so loud," Danny said, looking around. "Warm me up quick."

Mickey frowned. "What's the hurry? Zoom's here. Which means you won't pitch until at least the fifth inning— unless he just loses it and somehow blows up."

"I know," Danny said. "I just want to see if"—he checked again for eavesdroppers—"that pitch is still working."

"Ohhhh, *that* pitch!" Mickey said, even louder now. Danny clamped a hand over his mouth and led him away.

They went far down the sideline to a spot near a shady tree where no one could see them, and Danny began to throw.

Right away both boys could see that the new pitch was working just fine: stopping and dropping beautifully.

Danny was feeling more and more comfortable with it. All week long he'd practiced throwing it at his bounce-back net, which he'd moved to a new location in the backyard so as not to shatter another one of Mr. Spinelli's $200 windows.

Now Danny was eager to see how he'd do throwing it to real live batters.

He didn't have to wait long.

In the fourth inning, with the Orioles leading 2–0 and two outs, the Rays batter hit a hard comebacker to the mound. The ball caught Zoom squarely on his right shin before bouncing away.

He managed to limp after the ball and underhand it to Ethan at first for the third out. Then he dropped to the ground as if he'd been shot.

"Danny, get with Mickey and warm up!" Coach shouted as he ran to check on Zoom.

After Danny loosened up and returned to the dugout, he could see that Zoom was done for the day. The bone wasn't broken, but he was wincing and icing a huge knot on his shin.

"You're going in!" Mickey whispered. "Showtime!"

Can't wait, Danny thought. Though he felt bad for what had happened to Zoom.

"Wrap up the win for us, dude," Zoom said with a grimace. "Put a nice bow on it, okay?"

After the Orioles went down in order, Danny practically sprinted to the mound to begin the top of the fifth inning. As Katelyn passed him on her way to the outfield, she slapped him on the butt and said, "No pressure, nerd. Just their three-four-five hitters up, that's all."

Danny nodded and said nothing. This was no time to let Katelyn's big mouth get to him.

He took a few warm-up tosses, lobbing some easy fastballs to make the Rays think that was all he had, that they'd hit him like a piñata.

As the first batter dug in, Danny could feel his heart

beating in his chest. His mouth was suddenly dry, too. I'm nervous, he told himself. But it's a good kind of nervous. The kind that makes you focus and concentrate, not hurl all over your cleats.

He took a deep breath and looked in at the batter.

Mickey was right: it was showtime.

Danny went into his windup, rocked, and kicked.

The ball floated to the plate harmlessly. He could see the batter's eyes widen. He could practically hear him thinking *You gotta be kidding! You're throwing me this slop? This is going over the fence, meat.*

Just as the kid swung, the ball wheezed to a stop and plummeted downward.

Mickey gloved it and yelled, "Way to go, D!"

The umpire shot his right hand into the air: strike one.

Now the batter stepped out with a puzzled expression. He glanced back at his dugout, as if to say, *Did you guys see that?* But his teammates were already gaping at one another. Yes, whatever that pitch had done, they had seen it, too.

From behind him, Danny heard murmurs from the Orioles. But he didn't want to look at them. Not just yet.

The next pitch he delivered was even more tantalizing than the first. Again, the kid swung violently. Again, he hit nothing but air as the ball died on him and plopped into Mickey's mitt.

Strike two.

Now there were more quizzical looks from the Rays, louder murmurs behind Danny. He could hear a buzz coming from the stands, too. He wondered what his mom was thinking. With my luck, he thought, she went to the concession stand for a Diet Coke and missed all this.

The Orioles could see how frustrated the batter was now. He dug in again and banged his bat noisily on the corner of the plate. Then he held it high and waved it in menacing little circles, scowling at Danny the whole time.

Kid, making dumb faces at me isn't going to help you, Danny thought. He couldn't believe how confident he felt. In a way, he had never felt *more* confident standing on a mound.

He went into his windup again, rocked, and kicked. This time the ball drifted to the plate on an even higher arc. It looked like something out of a slow-pitch softball game.

The Rays batter was practically looking up at the sky when he started his swing. But the ball dropped so sharply that the kid missed it by two feet, nearly corkscrewing himself into the ground in the process.

Strike three.

The batter threw his bat in disgust. Mickey whooped, held the ball up, and pointed at Danny.

Now Danny permitted himself to turn around and soak in the moment.

Sammy looked as if he'd seen a ghost. Katelyn stood slack-jawed, hands on her hips. Coach was smiling from ear to ear and pumping his fist.

"Whatever you're doing," Coach yelled, "keep doing it!"

Finally, Danny glanced at the stands and saw his mom on her feet, cheering wildly along with the rest of the

Orioles fans. Any second now, he thought, she'll pull out her phone and call Dad to tell him all about this. Even as Danny turned back to the game, he could see his mom reaching for her purse.

The rest of the inning seemed to go by in a blur.

He struck out the next Jays batter on four pitches, this kid taking the same violent swings as the first batter. On the third strike, the kid actually raised the bat over his head and swung like someone taking an ax to a piece of wood. Or someone wielding a mallet and trying to ring the bell at a strongman competition at the state fair.

The batter after that tried to coax a walk, ducking theatrically on Danny's first two pitches.

But after both were called strikes, he took a vicious hack at the next pitch and missed it by a foot for strike three, the bat flying out of his hands and crashing into the backstop.

In the dugout, Danny got jubilant high fives from the rest of the Orioles and a big hug from a hobbled Zoom.

"Keep this up and I'll be out of a job," the ace starter said.

"Never gonna happen," said Danny, with a huge grin.

"Nerd, what's going on with you?" Katelyn demanded. "Is this a case of alien abduction? The aliens snatched the old Gas Can Connolly and left a new and improved version in his place? Is that how you got that ridiculous pitch?"

"Whatever, Katelyn," Mickey said. "Just sit back and enjoy it. In fact, you could literally bring a lawn chair out to right next inning. The Jays won't even hit a loud fly ball off my man here."

Mickey's words proved to be prophetic. After the Orioles went down in order, clinging to the same 2–0 lead, Danny cruised through the Jays lineup in the sixth inning, too.

Spectators were now recording his new pitch with their smartphones, the winking lights giving the place a concert-like atmosphere in the gathering dusk.

He struck out all three batters he faced, each kid flailing away helplessly at a pitch that simply wouldn't stay still long enough to be hit.

When he walked off the mound after the third out, the Orioles surrounded him, whooping and pounding him on the back. In the stands he saw his mom beaming and waving with one hand, the other holding her phone to her ear—shouting the final score to his dad, no doubt.

For the first time all season, he felt like a real closer.

The Rays coach jogged by just as Danny was throwing his gear in his bag.

"Terrific pitching today, kid," the coach said. "I don't know what you were throwing, but whatever it was, it was *nasty*. My guys are still shaking their heads over that pitch."

In that moment, as he headed out to join his mom, Danny knew one thing for sure: he hadn't felt this good after a game in a long, long time.

The smell of his mom's cinnamon-and-vanilla pancakes—Danny's favorite breakfast of all time—wafted through the kitchen.

It was the next morning and he was still glowing over the way he'd pitched against the Rays.

Both his dad and Joey were listening with rapt attention as Patti Connolly went over the highlights of the Orioles' latest win and Danny's shutdown role, including a detailed description of the wondrous new pitch he'd unveiled.

"Oh, you should have seen it!" she said. "Dropping out of the sky like a rainbow! I mean, those Rays batters didn't even come *close* to hitting it! It was like watching someone trying to swat a bee with a golf club."

"The Rays coach even said it was nasty," Danny added. "He told me it left his hitters shaking their heads."

He hoped that didn't sound too much like bragging. But it wasn't bragging if all you were doing was stating a fact, right?

As he poured a small puddle of syrup on his pancakes, Danny couldn't stop smiling.

For the first time all season, everyone at the table was actually talking about one of *his* games. And the hero this time wasn't tall, handsome, can't-miss major-league-prospect Joey Connolly, but his shorter, far less handsome, and perpetually overlooked brother.

Unreal, Danny thought. Of course, it could all end if Joey throws a no-hitter or turns in some other kind of all-galaxy performance for the Marauders. But I'll enjoy it while I can.

When Danny's electric performance had been thoroughly dissected, Jim Connolly shook his head and patted his son's shoulder.

"Gosh, I'm sorry I missed it," his dad said. "Work's just been piling up lately. But it sounds like you were awesome, buddy."

"Sorry I wasn't there either," Joey said. "The movie was totally lame. *The Planet of the Apes: Final Showdown.* Remember that simian flu that was supposed to wipe out all of humankind? Well, it didn't.

"Spoiler alert: a hardy band of survivors battles the apes," he continued. "And even though both sides have missiles and tanks and stuff, in the climactic scene, they're fighting each other with swords! It felt like my IQ had dropped forty points by the time it ended."

Patti Connolly made a face. "Yech! More quality entertainment from Hollywood. What is this, the sixtieth *Planet of the Apes* sequel? And why bother to call it the *Final Showdown*? You *know* they'll come out with another sequel next year. With another showdown."

"I don't know, the apes got smoked in this one," Joey said. "After they get whipped in the sword fight, the few remaining survivors panic and take off on their Harleys. And civilization is saved."

"Wait a minute," Jim Connolly said. "The apes ride *motorcycles*?"

"I didn't say it would win an Oscar," Joey said.

Danny cleared his throat dramatically.

"Ahem, can we get back to talking about *me*?" he said as the others cracked up. "I think I'm a little more interesting than a Harley-riding ape. Okay, maybe not. That's a tough act to follow."

"Yes, let's get back to you," his dad said, still laughing. "So this new pitch you're throwing sounds like some kind of eephus pitch."

Danny looked up from his plate. "You've heard of an eephus pitch?"

"Sure," his dad said. "It's sort of the generic name they used to give to any slow, junk pitch. No offense, buddy. Quite a few guys have thrown them in the major leagues. Yu Darvish of the Texas Rangers throws one. Dave LaRoche threw it for the Yankees in the seventies. So did Bill 'Spaceman' Lee for the Red Sox. In fact, he threw three of them in the seventh game of the '75 World Series against Tony Perez of the Cincinnati Reds."

He took a sip of his orange juice and chuckled.

" 'Course, Perez hit the last one for a towering two-run homer that's still circling over Boston. And the Red Sox lost. When it's working, the eephus can make a batter look foolish. But when it's not working . . ."

"Don't jinx him, dear," Danny's mom said.

Jim Connolly smiled. "No, it sounds like what Danny's

throwing is even better than an eephus. Sounds like his pitch has way more 'drop' to it."

Joey stabbed another pancake from the platter in front of him and said, "So how'd you come up with this new pitch?"

Briefly, Danny recounted the details of the impromptu postgame tutorial from Mr. Spinelli, leaving out his advice that Danny stop playing ball and busting other people's windows.

"Wow," his dad said. "Old Man Spinelli, huh? Who would have ever thought he knew anything about the game, let alone played it?"

"Turns out he was a terrific pitcher in college," Danny said. "Played for the University of Maryland and dominated with that pitch. Then he quit. No one knows why. Mr. Spinelli's never really explained it, I guess."

For a moment, no one spoke, each of them thinking about what could possibly make a player with that kind of talent turn his back on the game so suddenly.

"Okay," Danny's dad said finally, "here's the most important question of all: What did Spinelli say about the new window I put in for him?"

"He said you did a good job," Danny said, exaggerating slightly. Why hurt his dad's feelings by telling him the old man said it was just an okay job?

Jim Connolly grunted. "He'd *better* say it was a good job. Took longer to replace than stained glass in a cathedral."

As soon as breakfast was over and the boys had washed and dried the dishes, Joey appeared holding a ball and two gloves.

"Let's go," he said to Danny. "I want to see this new top-secret pitch of yours. Who knows? If it really works, I might have to steal if off you."

As they burst into the backyard, Patti Connolly yelled, "Please, no broken windows! No angry phone calls from the neighbors! No police cruisers pulling up to the house!"

"See how much you're stressing her out?" Joey said, laughing. "What's wrong with you, kid?"

Quickly, he paced off fifty feet, crouched, and held up his glove for a target.

"Let it fly, bro!" he said. "Make the magic happen!"

Danny nodded. It was great to see his brother excited and not at all resentful over all the attention Danny was getting. But that was typical Joey. Now Danny wanted him to be as impressed with the new pitch as everyone else seemed to be.

Carefully, he cupped the ball in his glove and made sure the grip was right. Then he turned and fired.

Except "fired" wasn't exactly the right word.

The ball arced through the bright sunshine with all the speed of a gentle badminton serve. Joey followed it with upraised eyes. He watched it sputter and drop into his glove, a shocked look on his face.

He rose to his feet, grinned, and took off his glove.

"Beautiful," he said. "That's all I needed to see. Save the rest for when it counts."

Danny smiled.

Now that I'm a real closer, he thought, every pitch should pretty much count from now on.

It was the hottest day of the summer, and a thick haze hovered everywhere. By one o'clock in the afternoon, the community pool was packed with splashing kids and their sweaty parents looking to beat the heat.

With Coach having mercifully called off practice, Danny, Sammy, Hunter, and Katelyn were lying on towels in a shady spot near the lifeguard stand.

Suddenly Katelyn sat up and gasped.

"Look!" she cried. "There's something in the water! Something scary!"

The others jumped up and craned their necks to see.

"I . . . I don't know what it is!" she continued. "It's big and fat and slimy. And it looks, I don't know, almost *translucent.*"

She turned to Hunter and added, "By the way, *translucent* means light can pass through it, only you can't see everything clearly. I know you were gonna ask, nerd. And don't say you weren't."

Hunter gave her a dirty look and sat back down.

The others kept staring out at the pool. Finally, Katelyn shook her head and smiled.

"Ooops, my bad," she said. "That big, fat, slimy thing? It's only Mickey."

As if on cue, Mickey clambered out of the pool, grabbed a towel, and plopped down beside them.

"Why, Mickey," Katelyn said sweetly, "so nice to see you! In fact, we were just talking about you. But please cover up before you join us."

"Don't start, Katelyn," Mickey said. "It's too hot for your crap." He looked over at Danny and grinned. "Besides, I need to have a talk with my man Triple-K Connolly here."

"Well," Danny said, yawning nonchalantly, "if you want to be *totally* accurate, I actually had *six* K's against the Rays. Not that anyone's counting. . . ."

"I was talking about three in one inning!" Mickey said. "And my man here did it twice! What a feat!"

Danny smiled happily. Nearly a week had gone by, and Mickey and the rest of the Orioles were still buzzing over how he had shut down the Rays with an awesome pitch no one had ever seen before.

In a way it was weird, Danny thought, being the center of attention on a team where, just a few days ago, he'd been a fairly anonymous player. But it was a weird-*good* feeling, not weird-bad. He decided he could live with that.

Word about his secret new pitch was getting around to the rest of the league, too. A number of people who'd been at the Rays–O's game were posting smartphone video of it everywhere on social media.

In fact, three kids from other teams had already come up to him this afternoon to talk about the new pitch. And after gushing about it, all three had practically begged him for a tutorial on how to throw it.

To which Danny had replied, only half joking, "Guys, what part of *secret* pitch don't you understand? Does KFC share the Colonel's secret recipe with just anyone? Does Coke share its secret formula with Pepsi?"

Now Mickey turned to him and said, "Dude, you need a name for that new pitch. A killer name that sets it apart from all the others."

"He's right," Sammy said. "A name that will strike fear in all who hear it!"

"Excellent idea," Katelyn said. "Even if it *did* come from Mickey."

Hunter sat up excitedly.

"I know what we should do!" he said. "Post something on Facebook! Hold a contest, ask people to come up with cool names for the pitch! Open it up to everyone, not just our friends! We'd get some great suggestions!"

Katelyn shot him a disgusted look.

"Nerd, are you out of your mind?" she said. "We'd get, like, a zillion responses. And we'd have to go through them all, edit out the bad ones, and—no, forget that. That's insane.

"With the collective brainpower we have here before us—ahem, minus the boy who just brought up the Facebook idea, of course—we should be able to come up with a good name."

She pretended to tap a gavel on her knee and said, "The floor is now officially open for suggestions."

"If it helps any," Danny said, "apparently they used to call a pitch like that an eephus pitch. We looked it up, me and Mickey."

"Eephus?" Sammy said. "What does that even *mean*?"

Mickey shrugged. "No clue. It didn't say. Guess some guy called it that seventy-five years ago and it stuck."

"Well, it's just dumb," Katelyn said.

"And *way* too old-school," Sammy said. "I go back to the fear factor. We need a name that makes batters tremble. A name that says, 'Dude, here's what's coming. And there's not a thing you can do about it except swing your dorky little bat and take your K like a man and get your sorry butt back to the dugout right now!'"

The Orioles laughed so hard that it was a minute or two before anyone could speak.

"What about calling it the Soft Rainbow of Death?" Hunter said.

They all stared at him.

"Totally, totally lame," Katelyn said. "Like, lame to the one-millionth power."

"Plus it's too wordy," Mickey said. "*Soft Rainbow of Death?* We're not writing poetry here, H. This isn't a sonnet. We need a good, tight name."

Hunter wrapped his arms around his legs and went back to pouting.

"What about the Gravedigger?" Sammy said. "You know, like, 'Grab a shovel and start digging, boy. Because after this pitch, you're going six feet under!'"

Mickey furrowed his brow. "I don't know . . . isn't there a monster truck called Gravedigger?"

"Yeah, there is," Katelyn said. "Gravedigger might make the batter think he'll get mowed down by a runaway vehicle in the parking lot after the game."

Danny threw his hands in the air.

"Hey, it's *my* new pitch," he said. "Don't I get to suggest a name?"

"Be our guest, O Mighty One," Katelyn said, rolling her eyes.

"How about the Connolly Spinner?" he said. " 'Cause it spins and causes an effect that is—"

Katelyn looked at him as if he'd just whipped off his swim trunks.

"No!" she said. "No, no, and no! We're not calling it something dweeby—just 'cause you're so vain you need your name attached to it."

"The Silencer," Sammy offered. "It totally silences the other team's bats."

Katelyn appeared to mull it over. "Okay, not horrible. But we can do better. I know we can."

No more suggestions were immediately forthcoming. The sun was climbing higher in the sky now and it was getting hotter, and the splashing from the pool was becoming increasingly hard to ignore.

The shimmering blue water had never looked more inviting.

How long were they going to sit here trying to come up with a name for a stupid pitch?

"Okay, what about this?" Hunter said finally. "What about the Terminator? Like you're telling the kid at the plate, 'The bomb is coming, son! And your at-bat is about to be *terminated*!'"

The other four looked at each other. In the next second, they were grinning and fist-bumping each other.

"Love it," Mickey said.

"Perfect," Sammy said.

"Totally perfect," Katelyn said.

They looked over at Danny, who gave the thumbs-up sign.

"The Terminator it is," he said. "Nice pull, Hunter."

Katelyn stood and tugged at the bottom of her bathing suit. "Well, with that essential bit of business out of the way, it's time to get wet again."

She gazed at Hunter and smiled.

"You know something, nerd?" she said. "You're not nearly as dumb as you look."

Then she trotted to the edge of the pool and dove into the crystal-clear water.

Hunter stared after her.

"I'm not sure if that was an insult or a compliment," he said.

The other three nodded.

"With that girl," Mickey said, "you never really know."

There were days when Danny thought Eddie Murray Field was about the most wonderful place on the planet.

On those days, the grass looked greener than anywhere else, and the rich, red-brown infield dirt was raked so clean you could barely spot a pebble.

On those days, the pitching mound looked so perfect you didn't want to spoil it with your cleats, and the foul lines gleamed so brightly you needed sunglasses.

This was one of those days.

Gazing around the old ballpark in the moments before the Orioles would face the Tigers, Danny knew one thing for certain: he had never been more ready to play a baseball game.

The drive from home had taken just seventeen minutes, a world-record time for his mom, which he considered a good omen.

Twice he had glanced at the speedometer and seen that his mom was actually doing the speed limit of fifty-five on the Beltway, instead of her customary ten miles per hour slower.

Once off the highway, Patti Connolly had even breezed through a yellow traffic light instead of braking sharply the minute it flashed and sending everyone in the car lurching forward as she usually did.

"Mom!" Danny had cried appreciatively. "It's like you're in the Daytona 500! Who's sponsoring this car, Valvoline?"

Now she was off to watch Joey's game, along with another slew of scouts expected to be on hand to see the Marauders ace show his stuff.

Jim Connolly wouldn't be at the field for Danny's game either. He was out of town for the week, shooting footage of a huge pod of pilot whales that had been spotted off the coast of Massachusetts.

But Danny was fine with not having a family member in the stands this evening. He didn't care if there was some-one to wave to or not, or someone to cheer for him or look properly stricken if he messed up.

He wasn't going to mess up.

Not tonight.

Not the way he was feeling.

For one thing, his confidence had never been higher, courtesy of having a certain pitch in his arsenal.

It made him feel a little like an illusionist conjuring a brand-new trick—turning his assistant into a dancing ele-phant, say, or making half of the audience disappear—that completely blows people away.

For another thing, the weather was perfect for baseball,

with the broiling heat and humidity having been replaced by lower temperatures and drier air that seemed to turbo-boost everyone's energy. Then there was this: the Orioles were still in the hunt for a play-off berth, which made every game important and exciting down the stretch.

As Coach had explained in their pregame meeting, the league was superbalanced this year. No team was running away from the pack. All they had to do, Coach said, was keep up the good pitching and play heads-up ball.

"Everything else," he said, "will take care of itself."

At this, the Orioles had rolled their eyes and looked at each other.

"Dad," Mickey had piped up, "you're pulling out the Buck Showalter clichés again. That was a really *bad* one."

"I know, I know," Coach had said sheepishly. "But I can't be insightful, charming, and incredibly eloquent *all* the time, guys. Sometimes you gotta go with clichés. Hey, at least I didn't go with the all-time classics. Like say we've got to take it one game at a time. Or that our backs are against the wall. Or that we have to give it a hundred and ten percent."

"Nice of you, Dad," Mickey said. "Those would have made us hurl."

A few minutes before game time, Danny asked Mickey to help him warm up.

This had become Danny's new ritual. It was a way to check on the new pitch and make sure it was still wheezing and dying, even though it would probably be a good hour before he came on in relief of Zoom.

As the two boys began loosening their arms, Mickey said, "Whoa! Check it out!"

He nodded in the direction of the Tigers dugout, where it seemed as if every player was gathered on the top step, leaning against the railing and studying the Orioles pitcher and catcher intently.

Mickey chuckled. "Your rep precedes you already, D. It's like Zoom doesn't exist anymore. They don't care about the starting pitcher, the kid who can almost touch eighty on the radar gun. If they strike out against him, well, so what? That's to be expected with his stuff, right?"

He turned back to Danny. "But you . . . *you* could embarrass the crap out of them. If they strike out against you and that filthy new pitch of yours, they *know* they'll look stupid. And someone will post video of it somewhere and they'll end up looking even stupider—if that's even a word.

"My suggestion?" he continued, staring at the Tigers. "Don't show 'em anything right now. Why give them a sneak preview?"

Danny nodded. As usual, the big catcher was giving him great advice.

Mickey was thirteen years old, but sometimes he could seem wise beyond his years, especially when it came to ball. At times like that, Mickey even *sounded* older, adopting his smoother and deeper "dad voice."

"No, they're not getting any free looks at your stuff," Mickey went on, waving pleasantly to the Tigers, who waved back. "Then, after Zoom destroys them with heat for four innings, you drop the Terminator on 'em and *crush* any chance of a comeback."

The Terminator.

Danny still couldn't help smiling every time he heard it. It really *was* a great name for the pitch—he had to give Hunter props. And Mickey was right: any lineup facing Danny's slow junk after Zoom's blistering fastball would be discombobulated, the batters' timing thrown off so badly they might never get it back.

"You guys will tear this league up!" Mickey crowed. "You'll go together like Batman and Robin. Like Bert and Ernie! Like peanut butter and jelly! Like macaroni and cheese. Like—"

"Yin and yang!" said Coach, who had wandered over to watch Danny throw.

The two boys looked at him blankly.

"Yin and yang," Coach repeated. "It's from Chinese philosophy. Explains how seemingly opposite or contrary forces can actually complement each other. Like light and darkness, fire and water, men and women, etc."

Whatever, Danny thought as he continued to loosen up. You want yin and yang? Wait till everybody sees the little surprise I've got planned for tonight.

The plan, Coach said, was to have Danny pitch three innings today instead of his usual two.

"Let's see how the new pitch holds up over a longer outing," Coach added. "We'll need to know for the play-offs, right? Could affect our strategy on who we pitch when."

But the wait to relieve Zoom seemed to take forever.

Danny played the first two innings in left and even contributed a base hit when the Orioles took a 2–0 lead in the second inning on Mickey's single and Ethan's inside-the-park homer over the center fielder's head. In the dugout after that, though, Danny was so amped he could hardly sit still.

But finally he was jogging out to the mound in the fourth inning, looking and feeling poised and confident.

Like a closer *should*, he thought.

At the sight of the new pitcher, a ripple of excitement seemed to go through the crowd.

Moms and dads and grandparents who moments earlier had been chatting idly or checking their smartphones suddenly started paying attention to the game. Little kids who'd been dashing about the nearby playground now seemed to materialize along the chain-link fence, gazing at the field expectantly.

Showtime once again, Danny thought as he watched the first Tigers batter step in. Only this time, they'll get an added entertainment bonus.

All week long he'd been secretly practicing a new and improved version of the Terminator in his backyard. He hadn't even told Mickey about it yet. Or Coach, for that matter.

The Terminator 2.0, he was calling it. And it was wild. The key difference was that this pitch had a much higher arc on its way to the plate. A ridiculous arc. And it *still* dropped like it had an anchor tied to it.

It reminded Danny of the pitches he'd seen in home videos of his dad playing slow-pitch softball in an unlimited-arc league, soaring pitches thrown by men with beer guts and bushy mustaches and bad mullets.

Staring in at the Tigers batter, he got the sign from Mickey, rocked, and delivered.

Immediately there was a gasp from the stands.

The ball climbed high in the sky, higher than anyone had ever seen a baseball pitch thrown, and it seemed to hover there for a moment.

The kid at the plate, Mickey, and the umpire all craned their necks upward at the same time, almost in slow motion. But as the ball descended, the expression on the batter's face changed quickly from dazed to frantic.

Danny could see him trying to decide: Swing or not?

At the last minute, he lunged at the pitch with a hurried, choppy swing. But by then the ball had already dropped into Mickey's mitt with a loud *THWACK!*

For a moment, the little ballpark was silent. Then the fans in both bleachers shot to their feet in unison like a startled school of fish, whooping and high-fiving in disbelief.

Behind him, Danny could hear the Orioles react with astonishment, too, laughing and cheering. Mickey pointed at him and fired the ball back with a big grin on his face. Even the umpire was smiling.

About the only one who didn't seem to find it entertaining was the Tigers batter.

Clearly shaken, he stepped out and took a weak practice swing. Then he peered into the dugout, where his teammates looked on slack-jawed. In the third-base coaching box, the Tigers coach threw up his hands as if to say, *I got nothing for you, kid. Never seen anything like it, either.*

After swinging futilely at two more mile-high

Terminators, the kid slinked back to the bench, muttering to himself. And when the next two batters struck out on equally baffling pitches, Danny jogged off the mound to wild applause from the Orioles fans.

Mickey greeted him on the top step of the dugout.

"What the heck was *that*?" he said. "Are we changing the name of the Terminator to the Rainmaker? Those pitches looked like they scraped the clouds!"

Danny nodded and sat down.

"Yep," he said. "Might be able to go even higher."

"No way!" Sammy said. "Any higher and it goes into orbit!"

As the three exchanged fist bumps, Danny beamed. He was still smiling forty minutes later, when he struck out the final Tigers batter to nail down the Orioles 4–0 win, the kid taking out his frustration by tomahawking the plate with his bat.

"Not a bad line you had today, D," Coach said, looking at his scorebook. "Nine batters faced, eight strikeouts, and a one hit-batsman. Which we know was complete bull."

It sure was, Danny thought. Instead of swinging wildly and striking out like the rest of his teammates, the kid had chosen to stand there and get plunked on the arm by a pitch that was slightly inside.

Coach had protested that the batter made no effort to avoid the pitch. The ump had disagreed. Or maybe he was just feeling sorry for the Tigers. But Mickey had made the whole argument moot by promptly picking the Tigers runner off first base.

All in all, Danny thought, not a bad debut for the new Terminator.

"Nerd," Katelyn said, "whatever the aliens have done to you, I hope they keep it up."

"Me, too," Danny murmured. "More than you'll ever know."

The reporter from KidSports TV and her camera-man were set up near the first-base dugout when Danny and Mickey arrived in their Orioles uniforms, bright orange jerseys and gleaming white pants.

It was two weeks later, and Danny was still on a roll with his special pitch. The O's had won their last three games and their dominant new closer had slammed the door on a potential rally in each win.

Not only was the Terminator the talk of the league, but video clips of Danny throwing it and batters taking hilarious swings at it had gone viral, attracting a flood of media attention and Internet buzz from all over.

Already this week, he'd been interviewed by the local newspaper, posed for a photo shoot for *Youth Sports Showcase* magazine, and done Skype chats with teen journalists from baseball-crazy Japan and the Dominican Republic, a translator haltingly relaying each question to the young American phenom.

Now he and the TV reporter, who introduced herself as Jessica Parker Lewen, sat in twin folding chairs in the bright sunshine at Eddie Murray Field as the cameraman prepared to shoot.

"Stand by . . ." Jessica said. She flicked the hair from her face with a toss of her head and smoothed her eyebrows with a delicate pinkie.

Danny guessed Jessica to be about sixteen years old. She had the whitest teeth he had ever seen, ringed by red lipstick that made them seem like two rows of glittering pearls set in a ripe tomato.

He wanted to ask what she did to get her teeth so white, whether it was the result of brushing, like, eighty-five times a day or using those teeth-whitening strips that seemed to be advertised every five seconds on TV.

Or maybe she was just one of those kids who never, ever ate or drank anything that could possibly stain them.

But before he could ask, the camera winked on and Jessica launched into her introduction.

"Thirteen-year-old Danny Connolly was, by his own definition, just an 'average ballplayer' until recently. But now he's perfected a mysterious new pitch that's made him the hottest reliever in the Dulaney Babe Ruth League.

"The pitch, which he calls the Terminator, has proved to be virtually unhittable since he first unveiled it a few weeks ago. And it's a major reason why the Orioles are poised to make the play-offs for the second straight year.

"Now he's our special guest on this week's segment of . . . *KidSports Rising Stars*!"

She turned to him and flashed a dazzling smile. "Danny, welcome to the show. Thanks for taking time from your busy schedule to be here."

Busy schedule? Danny thought.

It wasn't like he was the CEO of Bank of America. All he had planned for today was another round of blasting the bad guys menacing Spider-Man.

"Well, let's get right to it," Jessica continued. "Tell us how you came to develop such an incredible pitch."

Danny related an abbreviated version of the postgame pitching lesson he'd gotten from Mr. Spinelli, back when the O's reliever was at his lowest point, blowing games with alarming frequency and ticking off his teammates.

He followed that with a brief history of what was originally called the "eephus" pitch. Then he explained that, after much tinkering and hard work, he had come up with an even deadlier and more effective version of the Terminator.

This one had a considerably higher arc, he explained, something he'd been experimenting with lately.

"And you call this new version of the Terminator . . . what?" Jessica asked.

"Son of Terminator," Danny said, having decided Terminator 2.0 was too wonky and predictable.

In the background, he could hear Mickey snicker.

"And there could be a Son of Terminator Two," Danny added, "if we can make the pitch do anything else: somersaults, barrel rolls . . . I'm still experimenting."

For a moment, Jessica seemed to weigh the enormous implications of that statement.

Then, in an earnest voice, she said, "I know this is a lot to ask, but . . . would you demonstrate the pitch for our viewers? Please? It would really be a *huge* thrill."

She made it seem like if he didn't do it, the entire KidSports viewership would weep uncontrollably at the missed opportunity to see a once-in-a-lifetime phenomenon.

"Sure," Danny said. He removed the microphone that had been clipped to his jersey. Then he nodded to Mickey, who had already scooped up his mitt and was making his way to the plate.

Once on the mound, Danny went into his windup and floated the new version of the Terminator into the ether.

This one rose dramatically, like a hot-air balloon, higher than he had ever thrown it, before it suddenly stopped and plummeted into Mickey's mitt.

Quickly, the cameraman panned to Jessica, who gasped as if she'd just seen an alien spacecraft land at her feet.

"Oh, my gosh, that was totally awesome!" she cried. "Did we get that whole thing on video, Lars? Please tell me we did!"

Wordlessly, the cameraman gave her the thumbs-up sign and continued taping.

"That was a totally sick pitch, dude!" Jessica shouted to Danny. She scurried out to the mound with her hand-held mic to give him an awkward high five, still shaking her head in wonder.

"Okay, one final question," she intoned. "And this is the one *everyone* wants to know, the one that's number one on our 'McDonald's Top Ten Questions for Danny Connolly' survey. . . ."

She lowered her voice dramatically. "Danny, exactly *how* do you throw this new pitch of yours?"

Danny paused for a moment and grinned. He had prepared for this all morning.

"Well, Jessica, I'd like to share that with you and your audience," he began coyly. "I really would. But it's top secret. And if I told you, I'd have to kill you."

Jessica threw her head back and roared with laughter, as if this was the funniest thing she had ever heard.

"Oh, you're too much!" she cried. "Lars, isn't he just too much?"

Another silent thumbs-up from the cameraman confirmed that, yes, Danny was just too much.

When Jessica finally composed herself, she looked into the camera and intoned, "Danny Connolly: an interesting guest, to say the least. This has been Jessica Parker Lewen on this week's edition of *KidSports Rising Stars*.

"Join us next week when we talk to Jeremy Burnett, a rising star on the junior table tennis circuit, who has asked the world governing body of the sport for permission to play with a dinner plate instead of a paddle. So long for now."

As soon as the camera winked off, Danny heard a hollow clapping sound behind him. He whirled around to see Sammy and Katelyn leaning against the fence, rolling their eyes.

As Jessica and her cameraman went off to pack their equipment, Katelyn ran toward him holding a pen and a piece of paper.

"Oh, Mr. Connolly, you're my favorite player of all time!" she cried breathlessly. "Could I get your autograph? Better yet, would you sign my arm? If you do, I'll never wash it again, promise! I'll let it get so filthy they'll sign me up to do a soap commercial!"

"Okay, okay," Danny said. "How long have you guys been here?"

"Long enough to hear about your busy schedule," Sammy said with a grin. "We had no idea about your many, ahem, commitments."

"Nerd, I thought I was gonna gag!" Katelyn said. Here she mimicked Jessica's breathless, high-pitched voice. " 'Oh, Danny Connolly, you're too much! Isn't he just too much, Larsy?' "

"Haters gonna hate," said Mickey, who had just joined them.

He draped an arm around Danny and said, "I thought Jessica did an excellent job of bringing out the complicated side of a young pitcher struggling to find his identity on the mound in this fast-paced world of ours."

"Oh, puh-leeze!" Katelyn said. "Complicated? The kid's about as complicated as chalk."

"So the interview airs on this weekend's show?" Sammy asked.

"Remind me to watch something else," Katelyn said. "Like a documentary on the chemical properties of zinc."

Danny gazed at Katelyn and nodded sympathetically.

"Don't be jealous just because I'm famous and wildly successful," he said. "I'll still talk to you in the dugout. I'll still say hello when we pass each other in school. And a couple years from now, when you try to talk to me in high school and my bodyguards block you, I'll say, 'No, it's okay, guys. It's just ol' what's-her-name! The one who was on the Orioles the year I dominated.' "

Katelyn shot him a death glare.

"Nerd, you are really getting on my nerves now," she growled. "I'd suggest you cease and desist before—"

"You're right, Mickey." Danny smiled benignly and looked at his catcher. "It's turned into a hate fest. But that doesn't mean we have to stay here and be a part of it. Let's go."

As they turned to leave, the last thing Danny saw was a furious Katelyn lunging at him as Sammy held her back.

"You're getting out of here just in time, dude," Mickey whispered. "If she breaks free, she'll kill you."

Danny grinned.

"And if she can't get to me, she'll kill Sammy," he said.

"That girl could use an outlet for her aggression," agreed Mickey.

"Problem is, she already has one," Danny said. "It's called baseball."

17

It was a hot, sultry weekend evening at Camden Yards, and Danny and his family were part of the sellout crowd on hand to see the Orioles play the Red Sox.

It was a battle of two contending teams in the final two months of the season, and this alone was exciting. But more than anything, Danny was hoping to see his idol, Orioles closer Zach Britton.

He loved the way Britton entered the game, with AC/DC's "For Those About to Rock (We Salute You)" blasting over the PA system as he jogged confidently to the mound.

He loved the nonchalant way the big lefty went to work, too. Like, ho-hum, it was no big deal being asked to preserve a nail-biting 3–2 lead in the ninth inning with forty-five thousand people in the stands and millions more watching on TV.

Danny's dad called Britton's attitude a "lunch-bucket mentality," meaning he showed up every day to do his job, to do what was expected of him. And now that Danny was an actual member of the closer fraternity—okay, on a much smaller and less pressurized scale—he hoped to develop that kind of mental toughness, too.

Jim Connolly had scored outstanding seats behind home plate, but the family's first stop was the concession stand.

When they reached their seats with their hot dogs and sodas, Joey nudged Danny.

"Wait for it . . ." he whispered.

Patti Connolly didn't disappoint.

"Can you believe these ballpark prices?" she began. "They're really getting ridiculous. A Polish sausage for seven-fifty?! A pit beef sandwich for ten-fifty?!"

"Now comes the good part," Joey murmured.

"I remember going to ball games and paying a dollar for a hot dog," his mom continued. "And fifty cents for Crackerjacks. And the same for a Coke."

The two boys exchanged knowing grins.

"That was back when you had to walk ten miles a day to school, wasn't it?" Joey said.

"Through six-foot-high snowdrifts, right?" Danny added.

"Then, when you came home," Joey continued, "you had to milk the pigs and slaughter the cows. Or however that routine went."

"Right," Danny said, "and knit all the clothes for the family, wash the dinner dishes in the stream behind the log cabin, and do your homework by candlelight before throwing water on the fire and going to bed."

As the two brothers cracked up and exchanged fist bumps, their mom scowled.

"I'm so glad that I'm an eternal source of amusement for you two," she said. "Let me know when you're done making fun of your poor old mom."

Jim Connolly chuckled and said, "Honey, let's face it, you *do* go into the same rant about prices every time we come here."

"Oh, so now I'm predictable, too!" Patti Connolly wailed, crossing her arms across her chest and pretending to be insulted. But within seconds she was munching on her hot dog and happily absorbed in the game.

It confirmed what Danny had known for years: there was no way anyone could stay in a bad mood at Camden Yards, the greatest ballpark in the whole country.

The Orioles took a 3–0 lead in the early innings on home runs by Adam Jones and Chris Davis. But Boston battled back to 3–2 in the seventh, giving life to the usual hundreds of loyal Red Sox fans in the stands who seemed to follow the team everywhere.

Danny himself felt ambivalent about the Red Sox comeback, which was hard to explain to others.

As a die-hard Orioles fan, he could never bring himself to root for anything good to happen to the other team. But a tight game significantly increased the chances of seeing Zach Britton, since the big closer was only used by manager Buck Showalter in a save situation.

With the score still 3–2 Orioles in the ninth inning, Danny got his wish.

The outfield doors swung open, and as the Orioles fans rose to their feet and cheered, out came Britton in his gleaming white uniform, carrying his black glove like, well, a lunch bucket.

Like he was a factory worker reporting for his shift. Another day, another dollar. No big deal.

Britton went right to work and struck out the Red Sox lead-off batter, Dustin Pedroia, on a hard slider that totally handcuffed the Boston second baseman.

Jim Connolly tapped Danny on the shoulder.

"Look at the way Zach goes after them," his dad said admiringly. "No wasted motion. Waits patiently for the sign, goes into that little windup, and fires. No wasted *emotion* either.

"He's not jumping up and down and screaming and pumping his fist on every pitch," he continued. "He realizes you save a lot of energy by not getting all wound up out there. Your brother's like that, too. Just goes about his business and gets it done."

Joey, modest as always, blushed at the praise. But Danny knew his dad was right. *Don't get too high or too low when you're out there on the mound*—that was the mantra his dad had preached to both boys as far back as Danny could remember.

When Britton got slugger David Ortiz to ground out weakly for the second out, the crowd began clapping rhythmically as the Red Sox cleanup hitter, Hanley Ramirez, dug in.

Ramirez never had a chance.

He swung futilely at three straight fastballs, the last one seeming to rise until it finished at eye level, with Ramirez missing it by a foot.

As the ballpark erupted in noise, Danny kept his eyes locked on Britton.

A flashy closer like the Mariners' Fernando Rodney finished off wins by pretending to shoot an arrow into the sky. It was a move that didn't always sit well with opposing teams, who often felt like he was showing them up.

Other closers, Danny knew, pointed to the heavens and tapped their hearts, or did a little dance, or pumped their fists and pounded their chests.

But all Britton did was take a few steps off the mound and exchange a handshake and a hug with his catcher, Matt Wieters. Then the two joined the rest of their teammates, who were already lining up to slap high fives.

As the Orioles fans celebrated all around him, Danny found himself thinking again about his newfound success with the Terminator.

Could a kid who throws a big, looping junk pitch ever be considered a true closer?

Or were closers only big guys with 95-mph fastballs and late-breaking sliders who came in and blew away the other team with hard, intimidating stuff?

And even if he, Danny Connolly, ever got good enough to close out games in high school or college, could someone throwing a soft pitch that looked like it originated in fourth-grade recess ever get away with a hard-core entrance song like "For Those About to Rock"?

Danny wasn't sure.

"But I'd love to find out," he said to himself as the music blared and the fans danced and the big ballpark began to empty.

In one way, Danny decided, everything that was happening to him felt like a dream. But in another way, it didn't seem fair.

After all, Joey was the one with all the real talent in the family.

Joey was the one with the sizzling fastball, the curve ball that could buckle a hitter's knees, and the sweet, perfectly disguised changeup that had batters swinging for what seemed like half an hour before it reached the plate.

Joey was the pitcher with the big-league work ethic and mentality, a kid who never seemed to get rattled, with a future as bright as any schoolboy pitcher in the whole country. Not to mention that he was good-looking, kind, brave, and had every other positive physical and character trait you could name.

And yet . . . Danny was the Connolly brother getting the most attention now.

All because of a garbage pitch that an octogenarian had taught him—and one the old guy could still throw, too!

No, Danny decided, that wasn't even *remotely* fair.

Not that he wanted to go back to the old days, when everything around the house was Joey, Joey, Joey, and his own sports exploits, such as they were, didn't seem to register on his parents' radar.

But the idea that he and Joey would be out somewhere—the mall, the ice cream stand, wherever—and little kids would ask to take a selfie with Danny while all but ignoring Joey—that was so weird as to be beyond comprehension.

All this was running through his mind two days later as he and Mickey shared a pizza at Al's Italian Village after practice.

Mickey was devouring his second slice at his usual world-record speed. Watching him eat was a favorite ritual of the Orioles. Katelyn likened it to watching a bear devour a salmon plucked from a stream, only the bear had better table manners.

Suddenly Mickey stiffened.

"Don't look now," he whispered. "Table all the way in the back, by the door. It's Lord Voldemort."

Danny turned and spotted Reuben Mendez right away.

With him were three members of his Yankees posse. In between stuffing his face with a huge meatball sandwich, Reuben was regaling his boys with what must have been the funniest joke of all time, judging by the uproarious laughter and loud table-banging taking place.

Mickey threw his hands up in frustration.

"Why is it that as soon as you tell someone 'Don't look now,' they immediately look?" he said. "Can somebody please explain that to me?"

Danny shrugged, his eyes still locked on Reuben.

Memories of their last meeting came flooding back: Reuben swinging at a low, impossible-to-hit pitch and yet somehow golfing it into the gap to drive in three runs. Then he'd taunted Danny with a cry of "Too easy!" that became a full-throated chorus from the Tigers as they handed the Orioles their most dispiriting loss of the season.

Mickey, meanwhile, was still philosophizing, somehow managing to talk with three-quarters of a slice of pizza stuffed in his mouth.

"I mean, if you tell someone 'Don't touch that' because it's hot, they won't touch it," he continued. "If you tell them 'Don't eat that' because it'll make them sick, they won't eat it. But tell them 'Don't look now' and they look every freaking time."

He took another savage bite and mumbled, "There has to be a scientific explanation for that."

At that moment, Reuben looked up and noticed Danny staring at him. He pointed at the O's pitcher with the soggy remnants of his sandwich, causing the rest of the Yankees to turn and look, too.

"Oh, great! Way to be subtle," Mickey hissed. "You just guaranteed us a visit from the Dark Lord and his Death Eaters."

The visit came even sooner than expected.

Danny was reaching for his soda a moment later when he saw Mickey's eyes widen. Turning to his left, he found Reuben leaning casually against their booth, a toothpick jutting from his mouth.

The other Yankees were arrayed behind him, posing

with arms crossed and sullen expressions like wannabe rappers.

"What's up, boys?" Reuben said. "How's the pizza today? Everything good?"

Danny could feel his heart hammering in his chest.

But Reuben was smiling broadly. And his voice was soft and friendly, like he was the kid taking your order at the snowball stand.

"Hey," he continued, looking at Danny, "heard you got yourself a sick new pitch."

"Well," Danny managed to squeak, "I don't know about *sick* . . ."

"No, man, don't be modest," Reuben went on. "*Everyone's* talking about it. Word is, no one can hit it. Is that right?"

"Oh, I don't know. . . ." Danny said.

"I hear dudes are hacking at it like *this*," Reuben said.

He mimicked a hitter flailing helplessly at a pitch high above his head and corkscrewing himself into the ground, a confused look on his face.

It drew chuckles from his pin-striped posse, who quickly switched back to their hard looks.

"Ha! Sure, I guess there've been a few swings like that. . . ." Danny said uneasily.

He wondered where this all was going. Reuben, with his new running-for-mayor smile and nice-guy disposition, was more than a little creepy.

Even creepier than he was in full bully mode.

Suddenly Reuben leaned down until his face was inches from Danny's. The twinkle in his eyes was gone. The placid smile had vanished. His lips were a single purple gash, thin and menacing.

"You throw that junk to me," he growled, "I'll hit it so far you'll need a shuttle bus to go get it. You hear me?"

Danny recoiled involuntarily. What was that on Reuben's breath? he wondered.

Meatballs smothered in shredded cheese and marinara sauce?

Pepperoni plucked from one of his boys' pizzas?

Or an exotic blending of the two that, mixed with the kid's hot, stale breath, made the smell particularly rancid?

"We play you girls soon, right?" Reuben continued, gazing at Mickey now, too. "Like the end of next week. It's circled on my calendar. Can't wait."

He grabbed Danny's soda, took a long, slurping gulp, and slammed it on the table. The noise startled the couple behind them. Then he reached over, grabbed the slice off Mickey's paper plate, and took an enormous bite before tossing it back down.

With a last stare-down of both of them, he sauntered from the restaurant with his boys.

It was a good twenty seconds before Danny and Mickey exhaled.

"The ever-charming Mr. Mendez," Mickey said, "and his equally pleasant entourage. Always a pleasure to run into them."

Danny nodded. His mouth suddenly felt drier than it ever had, but he wasn't going to drink his Coke now. He noticed his foot was still jiggling uncontrollably.

"Good line about the shuttle bus, though," Mickey said.

"Wonder where he heard it? The kid's too much of a pea brain to come up with that on his own."

He looked down at the half-gnawed slice of pizza and smiled happily.

"At least he didn't eat the whole thing," he said, reaching for it. "So maybe he's not *all* bad."

Danny, on the other hand, no longer had any appetite.

Through the restaurant's large front window, he watched Reuben and his crew swagger down the street, pushing each other and laughing, seemingly unaware of the annoyed looks they were getting from everyone around them.

Despite his ever-growing confidence in the Terminator, Danny wondered how well he'd be able to throw it with big Reuben Mendez glowering at him from the batter's box and waving his big, shiny bat.

It looked like he wouldn't have to wait long for the answer.

Coach could get wired before games. When he did, his eyes would shine like crystal chips and he'd speak in little half sentences, almost as if his mouth had yet to catch up with all the thoughts pinging through his brain.

The Orioles had seen this act before.

Now, in the moments before they took the field against the Indians, they were seeing it again.

"Mission's simple," Coach said, pacing back and forth in front of them. "Win one of the next two . . . play-offs are right there . . . that *close*. Do it today. . . ."

"Dad, you're doing it again," Mickey said. "That thing where you sound like a robot. Or a video that's buffering."

"Sorry," Coach said. He flashed an embarrassed smile and took a deep breath.

"Okay, let's try that again," he said. "One more win and we're in the play-offs, kids. So let's get it today. We don't need the pressure of having to beat the Yankees next week, right?"

"Especially not with twenty-seven-year-old Reuben Mendez in their lineup," Katelyn cracked.

"Hey, that's not fair," Ethan said. "He's only twenty-four. My brother saw him on the Beltway this morning, commuting to his job as a stockbroker."

Listening to this, Danny couldn't help smiling. Reuben as a stockbroker—that was a stretch. But Reuben as a leg-breaker someday—that was a little more believable. Especially after the pleasant encounter they'd had with the big guy at Al's the other day.

But all the joking around was a good sign, Danny knew. It meant the Orioles were loose and having fun, the best way to play the game. He couldn't ever remember them being more confident than they were now.

The fact they were playing the Indians certainly helped matters. The Indians were one of the weaker teams in the league. And the pitcher the Indians were starting tonight, Tony Magas, was wild and inconsistent, though he had a decent fastball.

As soon as the game began, Tony gave up two walks. Even so, he somehow made it through the first inning unscathed. But the Orioles jumped on him in the second, when left-fielder Spencer Dalton drew a lead-off walk and Ethan hit a two-run shot over the center-field fence.

For their part, the Indians could get nothing going against Zoom. The big right-hander's stuff was overpowering, smacking into Mickey's mitt with a loud *THWAP!* and rocking the big catcher back on his heels.

With the O's still up by two in the fourth inning, Coach

came to Danny and said, "I'm wondering if we should even use you in this game. We could give you a rest, bring Sammy in to mop up. Save you for the Yankees in case we—"

Danny shook his head vigorously.

"Coach, with all due respect, the Terminator's like a finely tuned machine," he said.

Coach rolled his eyes. *"A finely-tuned machine?"*

"Right," Danny continued. "And in order to keep it humming at maximum efficiency, it needs work. Otherwise the calibrations are thrown off."

"The *calibrations*," Coach repeated.

"Right. And tonight it's calibrated to be used for at least three innings. So you see the dilemma if you don't put me in."

Coach smiled and shook his head. "Son, you got some line of bull, you know that? A world-class line of bull, if you want to know the truth. Okay, go warm up. So I don't have to hear any more about finely tuned machines. And whatever the rest of that gibberish was."

"Thanks," Danny said, grinning and grabbing his glove. "It's so nice to have a coach you can reason with. An intelligent coach, a fair coach, a coach who's always willing to—"

"GO!" Coach said, laughing. "Before I throw up right here."

When Danny came on in relief of Zoom in the fifth inning, with the Orioles still leading 2–0, it was to chants of "DAN-EE! DAN-EE!" from the O's fans.

He felt as relaxed as he'd ever been on the pitcher's mound. In the past, the minute he knew he was coming into the game, he would feel his heart thumping and his right hand begin to sweat, even if it was a cool night.

But not this time.

This time he was so loose and focused it was almost scary, almost as if someone had hypnotized him and pointed him at the other team and growled, "Now go get 'em!"

The Indians lead-off batter was a short, painfully skinny kid who looked like he was only a couple of years out of T-ball.

As the kid made his way to the plate, Sammy trotted to the mound. He held his glove over his mouth, the way major leaguers did when they didn't want the other team to read their lips.

"I feel sorry for this kid," he said. "Don't toy with him, D. That would be cruel. Like tearing the wings off a butterfly."

Danny watched the kid dig in nervously, as if the batter's box was the absolute last place in the world he wanted to be.

Mickey put down four fingers and wiggled them, the new sign to give the Terminator some extra lift. Danny nodded, already going into his windup.

The ball felt great leaving his hand. He watched it climb and pause as if hitting the brakes, then begin its laborious, humpbacked descent.

The Indians batter started his swing.

Everyone could see it would be an awkward, looping

swing, full of hitches and starts, the kind of swing kids take when they haven't played baseball for very long.

From behind him, Danny heard Sammy snicker.

Until the kid hit a screaming line drive over Sammy's head that rolled all the way to the fence in left center.

Danny was stunned. It took a second or two to process what had just happened.

What?! Someone made contact with the Terminator? And actually got a base hit? How could that be?

But, yes, there was Corey retrieving the ball as it died against the fence. And there was Sammy, the cutoff man, waving frantically as Corey's throw sailed over his head. It reached Justin on one hop, but his slap-tag was too late to get the little skinny kid as he slid into second base.

The Indians dugout erupted as the kid scrambled to his feet and punched the air triumphantly.

On the faces of the Orioles, there was only shock.

"Forget it," Coach yelled to Danny. "You're fine! Let's bear down and get the next guy."

Danny nodded numbly. He walked around the mound rubbing up the baseball, trying to regain his composure.

Okay, he thought, *it's not as if you were never going to give up another hit. That's part of the game. That's why you have seven fielders behind you and an all-star catcher in front of you. And they're all wearing gloves for a reason.*

Still . . . the ease with which the little skinny kid had hit the secret pitch was disturbing. Apparently someone had forgotten to tell him he was supposed to be awestruck at the mere sight of the Terminator, after which the script called for him to take three feeble swings and slink quietly back to the dugout.

Instead, he was dancing off second base now, grinning madly and practically daring Danny to throw over.

As the next Indians batter dug in, Mickey shot Danny a warning look.

Forget that kid at second, the look said. *Don't play games with him. Go to work on the batter.*

Danny nodded. Message received. He was feeling a little too rattled to try to pick anyone off, anyway.

From the stretch position, he checked the runner once more and delivered. The Terminator fluttered to the plate again in its slow, semigraceful arc. The batter showed no signs of swinging.

The bat on his shoulder never even twitched.

Then Danny heard it, a frantic roar that startled him.

"HE'S GOING!"

Actually, they could probably hear it in Wyoming. It seemed as if the entire Orioles team and every single one of their fans in the stands yelled it at once. But by the time the ball finally wheezed into Mickey's mitt, the skinny kid had taken third base standing up.

He clapped his hands and stared at Danny, the grin even wider. In their dugout, the revved-up Indians were stomping their cleats and banging their bats against the concrete.

Danny was furious with himself.

What an idiot! he thought. You throw a big, slow lollipop of a pitch that takes forever to come down, of course they're going to try to steal.

Try to steal?

Heck, throwing it with a runner on base was like giving him a free pass. It was like holding up a big sign that said: WHAT ARE YOU WAITING FOR? NEXT PITCH = OPTIMAL CONDITIONS TO STEAL. If anyone should be seething right now, Danny thought, it's Mickey. Throwing out base stealers was hard enough for a catcher without his knucklehead pitcher having a brain fart and throwing a pitch that could be timed with a sundial.

But Mickey was crouched behind the plate again as if nothing had happened, chomping evenly on his bubble gum and offering a steady stream of encouragement to his pitcher, as he always did.

At least I can throw the Terminator now, Danny thought. As slow as the pitch was, there was no way the skinny kid could steal home before Mickey caught it and slapped the tag on him.

And if the kid was dumb enough to crash into Mickey and try to jar the ball loose—sure it was against the rules, but base runners tried it every once in a while anyway—well, that wouldn't work so well either.

Running into Mickey, Danny knew, was like running into a brick chimney with shin guards. The chimney didn't budge. Meanwhile, you, the runner, came away feeling like you needed to get to the emergency room—fast.

The noise from the Indians was even louder now.

As the kid at the plate stepped out and began taking

vicious practice swings, like he was about to hit the most titanic shot in baseball history, Danny felt himself getting even angrier.

What's wrong with this picture? he thought.

Just moments earlier, the Indians were quaking at the prospect of facing a pitch that darted from the sky like a deranged bat. Now they were swinging from the heels like it was the Home Run Derby.

That's downright disrespectful, Danny thought. And it's about to change this very minute.

He nodded grimly as Mickey put down four fingers again. This would be the best Terminator he ever threw. He checked the runner on third, took a deep breath, and let the ball fly, snapping his wrist so hard he could hear it click.

There! he thought. That one felt perfect! That one should drop like a car pushed off a cliff. . . .

But it didn't.

Instead, the batter turned on it perfectly, drilling a shot down the left-field line that smacked against the fence and caromed away from Spencer for a triple.

Just like that it was Orioles 2, Indians 1.

Both Mickey and Sammy made a beeline to the mound.

"It's okay," the big catcher said soothingly. "Everything's perfectly okay. . . ."

"Absolutely okay," Sammy said, nodding. "There's no question that everything's okay."

"Totally okay," Mickey said, chomping furiously on his gum.

Danny looked from one to the other as if they'd lost their minds.

"Really?" he said. "Everything's *okay*? Because it doesn't seem okay to me, judging by what just happened."

"No, it's all good," Sammy said. "Just have to tighten up the Terminator, that's all. Make a couple of adjustments."

Danny ignored him and peered at his catcher. "What do you think the problem is?"

Mickey frowned. "I'm not exactly sure. It doesn't seem to be . . . *dropping* as much."

"Why isn't it dropping?" Danny said, hating the desperation that had crept into his voice. "I mean, that's the whole point, right? It has to *drop.* And it has to drop suddenly. Otherwise I might as well be lobbing the ball to these guys. *Underhand.*"

The umpire took a few steps toward them and yelled, "Let's wrap it up, guys. I'd like to get home before Jimmy Kimmel comes on, okay?"

Mickey turned back to Danny and said quietly, in his best "dad" voice, "Let's throw the Terminator to one more batter and we'll see what happens. It's such a sweet pitch, I'd hate to give up on it too early. If this next kid hits it, we'll rethink our strategy and go with something else."

Danny nodded gratefully as the meeting broke up.

Next to himself, there was no one on the Orioles who wanted the pitch to work more than Mickey, no one who better understood how a junk pitch could get in a hitter's head and completely mess up his timing—when it was working, anyhow.

Why wasn't it working now? That was the question. Danny could feel his chest tightening, the first waves of panic beginning to wash over him.

He tried to clear his mind as he peered in at the batter. The kid was standing tall and relaxed in the batter's box, looking supremely confident. Only his fingers folding and unfolding on the bat handle betrayed a hint of nerves.

Little alarm bells started going off in Danny's head. *This kid's a hitter. And he's patient, too. Probably will wait all day for his pitch.*

He took a last look at the runner on third, turned, and delivered.

The Terminator looked great as it bent toward the kid's shoulders.

Danny watched it and murmured, "Please drop, please drop. . . ."

In the next instant, he was whipping his head around as the kid hit a towering shot that cleared the fence in center field by ten feet.

Danny felt sick to his stomach. He turned back to the plate, where Mickey was watching the kid circle the bases and shaking his head in disbelief.

The big catcher was right, Danny thought.

It was definitely time to rethink their strategy—not that he could think of a backup plan at this very moment.

But before the Indians hitter had even finished his home-run trot, Coach bounded out of the dugout.

He waved his right hand in the air, like a man signaling for a taxi.

"Pitching change!" he yelled to the ump, pointing to

Sammy. "Danny, go to left. Tell Spencer to come in and play short."

As he passed his shell-shocked reliever, Coach gave him what was meant to be an encouraging smack on the butt.

It reminded Danny of what Buck Showalter did whenever he came out to yank a pitcher who'd just gotten lit up and was now hanging his head.

Keeping his face inscrutable, the big-league Orioles manager would give the pitcher a pat on the back while no doubt thinking, Son, you're killing us. You just flat-out *sucked* today. What am I going to do with you?

The rest of the game passed with agonizing slowness for Danny.

He was still numb forty-five minutes later when the Orioles failed to rally and lost 3–2. And he barely listened to Coach's postgame remarks, the familiar litany about keeping their heads up, sticking together, not pointing fingers at anyone, and blah, blah, blah.

"We still have a shot at the play-offs," Coach said in conclusion. "Let's forget about this one, okay? We're all about focusing on the Yankees now."

"The Yankees," Mickey said in a melodramatic voice. He slapped the bench for emphasis. "The *Yankees*," he repeated, this time making it sound like a dirty word.

Turning to his teammates, he flexed his biceps, scrunched up his face, and roared, "This I vow: The Yankees will feel our wrath! They'll pay for what happened today! And for the foul, despicable deed that they perpetrated on us last time!"

The Orioles cracked up—it was the perfect way to lift

the postgame gloom. Even Danny managed a weak smile.

But no matter what Coach said, Danny was pretty sure he wouldn't be forgetting this game for a while.

After gathering up his gear, he collapsed wearily on the dugout bench and leaned back, feeling the cool of the concrete on his neck.

One by one, his teammates tapped him on the knee or patted his shoulder as they drifted off, conveying the unspoken message: *Tough game. We know you feel like crap. Hang in there.*

Last to pass him was Katelyn, who leaned in close, as if she had something confidential to say.

She was so close he could smell her hair and feel her hot breath on his cheeks.

At first she seemed to be smiling.

But when he looked again, the smile had vanished.

"The Terminator," she whispered, "might have to be terminated."

Danny spent the night tossing and turning and having weird dreams. That often happened after he stunk it up for the Orioles. But it was even worse this time.

The feeling that he had let everyone down in a crucial game wouldn't go away. Nor would the feeling that his confidence in the Terminator was shattered beyond repair, lying in little broken pieces on the mound at Eddie Murray Field.

When he came downstairs the next morning, Joey was sitting at the kitchen table, looking glum. His laptop was open to his e-mail. Scattered in front of him was a huge pile of mail, all the letters he'd received from colleges and major league teams over the past few months.

As he stared at the blue screen, he sighed deeply.

"What's the matter with you?" Danny asked.

He grabbed a carton of orange juice from the fridge, checked to make sure his parents weren't around, and took a monster swig from it.

"Have to decide what I want to do next year," Joey said,

poking listlessly through the letters. "Can't seem to figure it out. . . ."

Danny snorted in disgust.

"*That's* what has you all worried?" he said, his voice rising. "Whether you're going to sign a pro contract and make millions? Or whether you're going to pitch for a great college team first, *then* sign a pro contract and make millions? That's the big dilemma here? Is that what you're telling me?"

Joey looked up sharply.

"Whoa! Someone wake up on the wrong side of the bed?" he asked. Then, after a closer look at his bleary-eyed little brother, "Actually, did someone even *go* to bed last night? You look awful, you know that? Absolutely terrible."

"No, don't try to spare my feelings," Danny said. "Give it to me straight. If I don't look good, just say so."

Joey sat back and folded his arms. "Okay, let's have it. What's bothering you?"

"Gee, I thought you'd never ask," Danny said.

He swigged the last of the juice and tossed the empty carton in the sink, where it rattled around noisily.

Then he sat down next to Joey and pursed his lips.

"Okay, here's *my* dilemma on this fine weekend morning," he began. "I have to decide whether I want to continue to suck at baseball—specifically, in this case, at pitching. Or should I just quit the stupid sport once and for all and join the marching band and take up, I don't know, the tuba—and possibly suck at that, too?"

He stared at his big brother.

"Now, of our two dilemmas," he continued, "you worried about riches and fame and pro ball and college scholarships, and me worried about generally sucking at baseball, which do you think is the most pathetic?"

Joey held up his hands in surrender.

"Okay, okay," he said. "Sounds like someone had a rough outing against the Indians."

"Yes, someone *did*," Danny said. "Therefore, that someone does not want to sit here and listen to you moan about your so-called dilemma. Which, by the way, is the equivalent of 'Let's see, do I want to go out tonight with Katy Perry or Kate Upton?'"

"Fine, we won't talk about me anymore," Joey said. "What happened to the secret new pitch? The one that was going to dominate hitters from now until eternity?"

Danny looked down at his hands.

"That's the million-dollar question," he said. "The Terminator wasn't terminating anyone, that's for sure. In fact, one of my teammates, who will remain anonymous—okay, it was that major butthead Katelyn—informed me that the Terminator should be terminated."

"It was that bad?" Joey asked.

"No," Danny said glumly. "It was worse."

Briefly he filled Joey in on the game against the Indians, the ineffectiveness of the secret pitch that he'd had such high hopes for, and the mocking he'd taken from the other dugout during their rally.

Joey listened attentively, then said, "How come Mom didn't say anything to me about this meltdown?"

"I started to tell her about it on the ride home last night," Danny said. "But she cut me off to talk about you."

When she'd described the Marauders' great win over the Beltsville Barons and Joey's latest suffocating performance—a two-hitter with eight strikeouts and no walks—Danny had gritted his teeth and kept silent for the rest of the drive.

"Man, I'm sorry," Joey said. "I told her that she has to stop gushing about me to everyone. It's embarrassing. But she's so into it! It's like she's my personal PR agency or something. But to lay all that on you after a tough game . . ."

Danny held up his hand.

"It's all right," he said. "She's proud of you. Dad is, too. I get that. We're *all* proud of you. But sometimes, when you have a tough night and all you hear is 'Joey did this' and 'Joey did that' . . . it kind of gets to you."

His brother nodded sympathetically. "So no theories on why the new pitch wasn't working?"

"Not really," Danny said. "It felt great leaving my hand. Mickey said it didn't seem to be dropping as much. But far as I know, I was throwing it the same as always."

"Maybe it'll come back just as suddenly as it left," Joey said. "Everybody goes through periods when things just aren't working—"

Danny emitted a mock gasp.

"*What?* The Golden Boy's had setbacks, too?" he said. "The one with the future that's all rainbows and unicorns had to struggle through something?"

"Very funny," Joey said. "You forget what happened to me on the jayvee team? I was no Golden Boy. There were lots of times when I couldn't get the ball over the plate. Just *couldn't* do it. But the coach didn't want to give up on me, 'cause I could throw hard."

His face clouded over. "So he kept trying to change my arm slot. One day he'd ask me to speed up my delivery, the next day he'd tell me to slow it down. He told me my leg kick was too high, then a week later he said it was too low.

"I was a mess. No control at all. And zero confidence. You don't remember that?"

Actually, Danny *did* remember that time. And the memory was still upsetting.

He'd gone to quite a few of Joey's games back then with his mom and dad. And Joey was right. It had been painful for the whole family, watching his big brother grow more and more confused and dispirited as the weeks went on.

Jim Connolly finally came to the conclusion that the jayvee coach didn't know what he was doing, that all the tinkering with Joey's mechanics was messing up his head as much as his ability to throw strikes.

Throughout the entire ordeal, Joey had never bad-mouthed the coach. And he had never whined about his misfortune to his parents or to his teammates. Each time he'd had a bad outing and the coach yanked him from the game, Joey's shoulders had slumped a little more and his worry had deepened.

But, invariably, by the next morning, the dark mood

was gone and Joey was looking forward to practice again, vowing to figure out what was wrong.

"Then one day—just like that—my control came back," Joey went on. "It was so weird, because it was during a game, too. I don't remember doing anything differently. But all of a sudden—*voilà!*—I could throw strikes again.

"It sounds corny, but it kind of taught me something," he continued. "Like patience. You go through bad stretches in baseball. Everybody does. Sometimes you just have to wait things out."

Danny grunted and shook his head.

Occasionally his brother could spout all this inspirational, rah-rah stuff and sound like an Under Armour commercial. And, yeah, sometimes it made you feel better about your own particular problem.

But this wasn't one of those times.

Right now the stuff about patience was getting on Danny's nerves.

"I've been waiting things out all season," he said, the edge returning to his voice. "Pretty much got lit up all season, too. Then I learn a new pitch, right? And it makes all the difference in the world.

"Then—*poof!*—it disappears after a few games! And they start hitting me again like I'm a piñata!"

He let out a low moan and ran a hand through his hair. "Tell me that's fair. . . ."

"No, it's not," Joey said. "But since when is baseball fair? It wasn't exactly fair to me on the jayvees. But you can't give up. Keep working hard and things will turn around. Just keep doing it. Sometimes it's that simple."

Danny couldn't take it anymore. Now his brother sounded like a freaking Nike commercial.

He was glad when Joey gathered up his laptop and mail and left.

I love the guy, Danny thought. But another minute of that and I would have puked.

The phone rang at one o'clock in the afternoon, just as Danny was readying Spider-Man for his big brawl with the supervillain Kraven.

He sighed and threw down the controller. He was still in a foul mood—all week long, he'd been trying to get the Terminator to work again, throwing it dozens of times a day to Joey in the backyard with zero success.

The name that flashed now on caller ID, Hunter Carlson, didn't make him feel any better.

"Meet me at the park in a half hour," Hunter said. "And bring your glove."

"Why?" Danny asked warily.

From past experience, he had found it was always good to be leery about anything Hunter proposed.

Sure, he'd come up with a great name for the Terminator. But he was also one of those kids who was always dreaming up elaborate schemes for getting out of schoolwork, getting out of baseball practice, getting out of *something*.

Except those schemes invariably backfired and got him—and whoever else was involved—in trouble.

"Trust me," Hunter said. "Think I have the answer to your problem."

"You have the tuba I'll be playing in the marching band this fall?" Danny said.

There was a pause on the other end.

"What?" Hunter said finally.

"Never mind," Danny said. He turned off the video game. "All right, I'm not getting anywhere with Spidey, anyway. He's looking totally lame against Kraven. See you soon."

When he got to the park, he found Hunter on the small baseball field where the younger kids played. With him was possibly the nerdiest kid Danny had ever seen.

The boy appeared to be about sixteen. He wore thick black glasses, baggy black shorts, and a black T-shirt that said: I CAN EXPLAIN IT TO YOU, BUT I CAN'T UNDERSTAND IT FOR YOU.

He was so pale that the veins running up and down his arms stood out like blue tentacles. At the sight of Danny approaching, he quickly looked down at his shoes.

"This is Elmo," Hunter said.

"Elmo," Danny repeated. "You mean like the—"

"Muppet," Elmo said, nodding but still not looking up. "Yes, unfortunately I was named after a furry red monster with a falsetto voice from a children's TV show." He paused. "My parents, you see, are a bit . . . *unusual.*"

What a surprise, Danny thought.

"Elmo's here to help you with the Terminator," Hunter said.

Danny studied Elmo again. This time he noticed he was

holding a small video camera. A calculator and notebook protruded from a pocket of his shorts.

"Do you play baseball, Elmo?" Danny asked.

Elmo looked up with a horrified expression.

"Oh, no," he said quickly. "I'm not very good at sports. You wouldn't want me on your team. All you'd have to do is take one look at the way I throw. And catch. And hold the bat.

"In gym class, I'm always the last kid picked. It doesn't matter what we're playing, either. Sometimes the coach will just randomly put me on a team, because no one wants me to—"

Danny held up a hand. "We get the picture. No need to go on."

"Elmo's the smartest kid I know," Hunter said. "He's studying . . . what is it again, dude?"

"Experimental physics," the boy said.

Hunter smiled proudly. "Right. Which of course is the study of, um . . ."

". . . physical phenomena," Elmo added helpfully. "To gather data about the universe."

"Right," Hunter said. "So you see where we're going with this."

Danny stared at both of them.

"Actually, I don't," he said. "I mean, it's great and all that Elmo's a high school physics whiz—"

"*College* physics whiz," Elmo said. "I'm, uh, technically still in high school. But I take advanced physics classes at the University of Maryland. My teachers said I wasn't being challenged enough in the sciences. I'm sure neither of you knows what that's like, but it can be quite flattering."

Danny felt himself doing a slow burn. He shot Hunter a look that said, *Is this dork for real?*

Turning back to Elmo, he said drily, "You're right, I can't imagine what that's like. But I don't need any help from you. Have a nice life."

He turned to leave, but Hunter grabbed him by the arm.

"Dude, don't you want to find out why the Terminator isn't working?" he said. "Huh? Well, desperate times call for desperate measures."

"Pretty sure I've heard that somewhere before," Danny said.

Hunter shrugged. "Look, you got rocked by the Indians, right? And you've been working on it all week and gotten nowhere. You *need* to fix that pitch. What do you have to lose?"

"Okay, you got me there," Danny said with a frown. "I have no answer for that. But I don't need Professor Weirdo here slipping on his white lab coat and examining me and talking in that condescending tone."

Hunter draped an arm over Danny's shoulder and led him away from Elmo.

"Okay, the boy lacks some, uh, social skills," Hunter said in a low voice.

"Ya think?" Danny said.

"But who cares as long as he can help you, right?" Hunter said. "Who cares if a doctor has a great bedside manner, as long as he prescribes the right medicine? Maybe that's what this kid's like. Will you at least give him a shot?"

Danny thought it over for several seconds. Finally, he sighed and said, "Okay, fine."

Which immediately made him even more depressed.

Unbelievable, he thought. This is how low I've sunk. I'm actually agreeing to get pitching help from someone who looks almost too geeky for *The Big Bang Theory*.

When they rejoined Elmo, Danny asked, "I'm almost afraid to ask. But exactly how is he going to help me?"

Hunter smiled and said, "Tell him, E."

"Certainly," Elmo said. He squinted up at Danny. "What I propose to do is shoot video today of you throwing your secret pitch. We'll measure the velocity of the ball approaching home plate, the angle of trajectory, rate of descent, your inverted arm-action ratio—"

"Inverted *what* ratio?" Danny asked.

"Please," Elmo said, holding up his hands. "It would take too long to explain. And even if you understood the metrics behind that—which you *wouldn't*, of course—"

Danny could feel himself getting steamed again.

"Uh, Elmo," Hunter said quickly, "maybe we could just skip the metrics and get to the important part. . . ."

Elmo nodded. "The data mean nothing without a base comparison level," he went on. "In the simplest terms, we'll compare the measurements that we get today to the measurements we get from old video of you pitching against, for example, the Rays. A game in which you dominated and the Terminator was at its most effective."

"Then," Hunter added, "maybe we can see what you're doing different now. And why you're kind of—no offense—sucking."

Danny's cheeks turned red. "Why would I take offense

at someone telling me I suck? You meant that as a compliment, right?"

"Okay, okay, don't get hot," Hunter said. "Elmo, uh, why don't we get started."

Hunter grabbed his glove and went behind the plate. Danny paced off a distance of fifty feet and marked it with a line in the dirt. Elmo set up with his camera a few feet to the right of the batter's box so it wasn't looking directly into the sun.

"And . . . action!" he said, staring into the lens.

Action? Danny thought. We're not shooting *Bad News Bears IV* here.

He warmed up by throwing a few lackluster fastballs. Then, for the next ten minutes, he threw the Terminator exclusively.

This time, the pitch felt strange leaving his hand. He could see the ball was doing very little as it neared the plate. The look of concern on Hunter's face deepened with each pitch. Elmo peered into the camera, blinking furiously, and occasionally turned away to jot down notes and punch figures into his calculator.

After ten minutes, Hunter waved and shouted, "That's enough!"

Shaking his head, he jogged out to Danny.

"Dude, I'm going to be honest with you," he said. "You came to us just in the nick of time."

"I didn't *come* to you, remember?" Danny said. "You came to me."

"Whatever," Hunter said. "The point is, your secret pitch

isn't doing anything. I mean *nothing.* It's not stopping. It's not dropping. There's no movement to it at all. It's about as hard to hit as a beach ball."

He popped a fresh piece of bubble gum in his mouth and chewed ferociously, his eyes locked on Danny's.

"If you bring that weak stuff against the Yankees," he said gravely, "they'll kill us."

Abruptly, he brightened. "But, hey, let's not worry about that now! We'll let Elmo work his magic with the video and the numbers and see what he comes up with. Then we'll get back to you."

He looked over to where Elmo was packing up his camera and scribbling a few final notes.

"I'm telling you," Hunter said, smiling, "that boy is a genius. Did I tell you what he got on his SATs? Listen to this. . . ."

But Danny was already zoning out, the rest of the story becoming so much white noise that really didn't matter.

Because he had already decided whom he'd turn to for help with the Terminator.

And it wasn't someone who looked like Sheldon Cooper's even-geekier brother.

It took Danny another couple of days before he finally got up the nerve to ring the doorbell.

For maybe twenty seconds, there was only silence inside the house.

Finally, a window on the second floor flew open and a voice yelled, "Unless you're with the lottery and I won the four hundred million jackpot, go away!"

Danny heard the window slam shut. He took a deep breath and rang the bell again.

Again the window was thrown open.

"So I *did* win the four hundred million? Okay, just slip the check under the door, then go away!"

Before the window could close, Danny sprinted down the porch steps and out into the sunshine so the old man could see him.

"Mr. Spinelli, I need to talk to you!" he shouted. "It's important!"

The old man looked down, shielding his eyes from the sun. He appeared to be wearing a painter's smock again.

But, mercifully, this one wasn't streaked with red paint, giving him the blood-splattered look of an ax murderer.

This one was covered with vivid splotches of aquamarine. With paint smeared on parts of his neck and face, he looked like a member of the Blue Man Group.

"Oh, it's you," Danny's neighbor said. "Don't tell me: despite your normally pinpoint control, you broke another window, right? You sailed another pitch over the fence, didn't you? And you're just getting around to telling me. . . ."

"No, nothing like that," Danny said. "I need some advice."

Mr. Spinelli glared at him.

"Who do I look like, Ask Amy?" he said. "Or whoever that wretched columnist is in the newspaper, the one who thinks she knows it all? Can't you see I'm busy?"

The window started to close again.

"Please!" Danny said, louder now. "You're the only one who can help me! It's about that pitch you taught me. It's . . . not working!"

Mr. Spinelli stared down at him for what seemed like an eternity.

"Front door's open," he said at last. "Come up to the studio. Second floor, big room to your right."

For an instant, he seemed to hesitate.

"But I'm telling you now, I don't have all day!" he yelled before the window slammed shut.

Danny let himself in and took the stairs two at a time. When he entered the studio, his jaw dropped. The walls were covered with paintings—row after row of artwork—and every single one had a baseball theme.

There were paintings of gloves so detailed you could

see every shadowy crack in the brown leather, and balls so lifelike that the red stitching seemed to jump off the gleaming white horsehide, almost inviting you to grip it.

There were paintings of bats, mostly old-school Louisville Sluggers, so painstakingly rendered that you could see the intricate swirls in the polished ash, maple, and hickory, as well as the shine on the handle, just above the knob, where a batter would grip it and wear it down over time.

There were paintings of famous old ballparks, like Boston's Fenway Park and Chicago's Wrigley Field, and newer ones like Baltimore's Camden Yards and New York's Yankee Stadium and Citi Field.

If there was any doubt as to who had painted them, each was signed *AS* with a bold flourish in the lower right-hand corner.

Seeing Danny's shocked gaze, the old man grunted.

"What did you expect me to paint?" he asked. "A dumb bowl of fruit? A basket of vegetables from a fall harvest?"

"I . . . I don't know," Danny said. "It's just . . . you said baseball was a silly game. And a waste of time." He swept his hand toward the artwork. "So I didn't think you'd be doing . . . *this*."

Mr. Spinelli walked over to a sink and washed his hands and face.

"Baseball *is* silly," he growled, reaching for a towel. "And it's a monumental waste of time." Then his voice grew softer. "But it sure has a way of staying with you. Long after you've finished playing it."

He stared out the window for a moment, lost in thought.

"But you're not here to talk about my art," he said finally. "What's this about a fresh new crisis in your young life? And don't give me a big song and dance about it. Give me the CliffsNotes version."

Quickly, Danny recounted how well he'd done with the Terminator at first, then how it failed him against the Indians, how it was still doing nothing during his throwing sessions in his backyard, how it had done even less when he threw it in the park to Hunter, with the supernerd Elmo taking measurements as if he were a NASA scientist.

Now, Danny went on, the big game against the Yankees was almost here. And he was panicking over not being able to contribute with the play-offs on the line.

When he was through, the old man nodded sympathetically.

"Boy, that's the dirty little secret about the pitch: it doesn't work all the time," he said.

Danny looked startled. "It doesn't?"

"No," he said. "Sorry to burst your bubble. That's why you have to mix it in with your other pitches. You can't just rely on that one. But if you really stick with it, put in the time and effort to master it, it'll work a *lot* of the time.

"And having something work a lot of the time in baseball isn't bad. Especially when you consider that the best hitters in the game make an out seven of every ten times at bat."

"But it's not working for me at *all*!" Danny said, hoping he didn't sound too whiny. "And the biggest game of the year is coming up!"

"Son, anyone ever tell you you're kind of needy?" Mr.

Spinelli said. "Okay, the first thing you do is make sure your fundamentals are sound. Go over the checklist: Are you holding the ball the right way? Are your fingers in the correct position? Are you snapping your wrist the way you're supposed to on the release?

"The other thing," he continued, "is that you don't want to grip the ball too tightly. A pitcher tends to do this when he's tense, when he's facing a pressure situation. I bet when the Indians started hitting you, you were squeezing that ball so tight you could have popped the stitching."

Danny knew the old guy was right.

At one point in the game against the Tigers, right before the kid homered off him, Danny had looked down and noticed he was squeezing the ball so hard his knuckles had turned white.

"But gripping it tightly is the worst thing you can do with that pitch," Mr. Spinelli said. "See, you have to throw it free and easy to make it drop. The guy who taught me the pitch said it should drop to the plate like a wet diaper."

Danny tried to visualize a wet diaper sailing through the air.

Then he tried to visualize the horrified expression on the face of, say, Reuben Mendez as he stood in the batter's box, watching this dripping mass of poly-fiber hurtling toward him before dropping with a thud.

The image made him smile.

Playing with wet diapers, he thought, could *really* liven up the game. Maybe we could pass that on to the rules committee in the off-season.

He looked at Mr. Spinelli and said, "You know so much

about pitching. And you're still passionate about it—I can hear it in your voice. So why did you quit your college team back in the day?"

The old man took off his glasses. Wearily, he massaged the bridge of his nose.

"You heard about that, huh?" he said. "Part of the reason had to do with exactly what you're going through. I had a great season, but I could never make the pitch work one hundred percent of the time. And I was a perfectionist—not a good thing to be when you play this game.

"I knew the hitters would figure me out eventually. My fastball stank. And my curve and changeup were strictly mediocre. The league was bound to get wise to this scared young pitcher relying too much on a junk pitch that wasn't always effective.

"Guess I couldn't face that. So I just walked away. It's something that bothers me to this day."

He looked down and scraped a splotch of paint off his fingernail.

"You said that was *part* of the reason you quit," Danny said. "What was the other part?"

The old man's eyes narrowed.

"What makes you think I want to share that with you?" he barked. "Jeez! Can't a guy keep anything to himself anymore? Is there no sense of privacy in today's society?!" He nodded toward the door. "Okay, your time's up. I'll walk you out."

Reluctantly, Danny followed him down the stairs. When they reached the porch, Danny paused.

"This is probably not a great time to ask this . . ." he began.

"Then don't," Mr. Spinelli said.

But there was no turning back now for Danny.

"No, I have to," he said. "Would you come to our game against the Yankees? It would really mean a lot to me."

"No," Mr. Spinelli said.

"*Please?* Just to see if I'm doing anything wrong with the pitch? It's like a totally must-win game for us! And you were at some of the earlier ones. . . ."

The old man shook his head. "If things go wrong, go over the checklist. Go over each and every item—again and again. You have to figure this out on your own, boy."

Danny's shoulders slumped. "Okay. Guess you can't blame me for trying."

When he reached the sidewalk, he turned and waved.

Mr. Spinelli was still standing there, watching him from the porch. He waved back and Danny thought he saw something else on the old man's face right before he went back inside.

Something he had never seen before.

It almost looked like a smile.

Almost being the operative word.

"Let me get this straight," Mickey said incredulously. "There's a *checklist* for throwing the Terminator now?"

Danny nodded.

"Finger positioning, grip pressure, wrist snap—they're all important, dude," he said. "Gotta go over each one."

"A *checklist*?" Mickey repeated. "Seriously? You're not launching the space shuttle! You're throwing a baseball!"

He shook his head and gazed out at the field, where the Orioles were loosening up for their final practice before playing the Yankees.

"The game used to be so simple," he continued. "See the ball, throw the ball. See the ball, hit the ball. See the ball, catch the ball. Whatever happened to that, huh? Whatever happened to the good old days, BC? Before Checklists."

"Gee, Grandpa Mickey, I'm not sure," Danny said, laughing. "Are you spending your days in a rocking chair on the porch, with a blanket over your shoulders? Yelling at little kids to get off your lawn?"

"Matter of fact, I *am* already yelling at little kids," Mickey said. "My dad has me mow the lawn, right? And afterward, it looks great. Then the little brats next door cut across it with their bikes. And sometimes they leave tire marks."

"Ooooh, tire marks!" Danny said. "What a bunch of thugs!"

He punched Mickey playfully on the shoulder and said, "You're, like, thirteen going on eighty, you know that? What are you going to be like when you're fifty?"

"It won't be pretty," Mickey agreed. "I'll be the crankiest guy on the block."

Danny finished stretching his legs and began windmilling his throwing arm to loosen it.

"Anyway, the good news is, there's a checklist to go over when the Terminator's not working," he continued. "The bad news is, the checklist hasn't helped. I've been throwing the pitch in the backyard all week. It's floating up there like a wet diaper. But it's not doing anything else."

Mickey looked alarmed.

"Floating like a wet *what*?" he asked.

"Never mind," Danny said. Silently he composed a memo to himself: not a good idea to share the wet-diaper analogy with your catcher.

"Mr. Spinelli said I have to mix it up, not just rely on one pitch," he went on. "Problem is, my other pitches suck right now. And they've sucked all season. That's why I really need the Terminator to work. Otherwise, if Coach puts me in against the Yankees, we could be in big trouble. And I'll be playing the tuba when school starts."

"That'll set tuba-playing back a hundred years," Mickey said with a grin. He grabbed a ball and his mitt. "But right now let's loosen your arm and not your lips."

As the two boys played catch on the sidelines, Danny couldn't believe how nervous he was.

Coach had agreed to let him start off throwing batting practice, to see if he could get the Terminator back on track. Who gets nervous about throwing BP? Danny thought. But he could feel the anxiety building and his throwing hand was starting to sweat.

Just like the pre-Terminator days, he thought. When seeing me on the mound was like Christmas morning for the other team. Only now it was his own teammates and coach he was trying to impress, at least enough so they'd have faith he could step up against the Yankees.

The Orioles took infield and outfield practice for the first twenty-five minutes, with Danny and Spencer splitting time in left field.

Finally, it was time to hit and Coach waved him in to pitch. As he warmed up with Mickey, throwing just easy fastballs, he went down the checklist for the Terminator, ticking off the things he needed to be conscious of.

It felt like cramming for an exam seconds before the teacher handed out the test papers, but he really had no other choice.

Actually, it felt like cramming for an exam with someone yapping in your ear, the way Katelyn was now as she stepped into the batter's box.

"Coach, are you sure you want this boy throwing to us?" she yelled. "Because the way I'm feeling today, he could get hurt! All right, nerd, bring it! And not that weak stuff you threw to the Indians the other day."

Danny could feel his face getting hot as the rest of the Orioles cracked up. Even Coach grinned as he stood off to one side, watching with his arms folded across his chest.

Sticking with his new vow to mix up his pitches, Danny started Katelyn off with a fastball, which she fouled off. She fouled off another fastball, too, and then popped up a third one. She let out a yelp of frustration and pounded the dirt with her bat.

"Nerd, you are so freaking lucky!" she shouted. "Throw another one of those so-called fastballs. *Please!* I'm begging you."

Instead, he threw the Terminator.

The perfect pitch for the wild-eyed, revved-up batter who's ready to swing out of her shoes, he thought. At least it was the perfect pitch when it worked.

He watched it float to the plate, watched Katelyn's eyes light up as she recognized the pitch, watched her left foot stride forward as she started her swing.

He held his breath . . . and felt his stomach sink as she smashed a shot down the right-field line. In a real game, it would have been a double—everyone watching knew that, too.

She smacked the next two Terminators he threw, too, both of them line drives that went screaming into the right-center gap. After her last swing, she flung her bat aside and pointed at Danny and cackled.

It was the same with the next three batters who stepped in. Ethan clubbed all three of the Terminators he saw to the deepest parts of the outfield. Danny threw only two of the junk pitches to Corey, who roped both into left field for solid base hits.

By the time Spencer dug in, it was obvious to everyone that the Terminator had zero drop to it, that it was hanging over the plate like a party balloon, begging to be smacked into the next zip code.

Danny had only to see the look of concern on Mickey's face and Coach's worried frown to know how bad things were going.

A moment later, Coach appeared at his side.

"Okay, that's enough for today," he said gently. "Don't want to overextend that arm. I'll take over. Why don't you grab a bat and take a few swings?"

So much for getting the Terminator back on track, Danny thought bitterly. Right now it was just a train wreck.

So much for the stupid checklist, too. Might as well start practicing the tuba.

He stomped off the mound and slammed his glove against the backstop with a loud *CLANG!* Then he reached down, grabbed a bat, and threw that against the screen, too.

When he turned around, the rest of the Orioles were staring at him. Coach gave him a long, hard glare, but said nothing.

"Great," Danny murmured to himself. "Now they all think I'm a nut job, too."

Just then a wild idea occurred to him.

Maybe the game against the Yankees would get rained out. That would give him another day or two to see if he could breathe some life into the Terminator, which right now looked more like a terminal case.

Ha, who am I kidding? he thought.

A great, gushing thunderstorm, complete with lightning streaking the sky, that would leave the field unplayable Friday?

I don't have that kind of luck.

25

There were times, Danny knew, when he needed to get away from baseball and clear his head.

There were times, as his dad always said, when the game could just chew you up into little pieces and spit you out. Make you feel like you had no business playing it and you were making a fool of yourself.

This was definitely one of those times.

Two days after the Orioles' practice, Danny wondered if he had ever felt more discouraged with his pitching. So when he got a text from Mickey that afternoon that read *We're going to hit at Grand Slam. Coming?* he was shocked to find himself responding, *Sure. What time?*

Why did I do that? he wondered, staring at his phone.

Do I love baseball that much?

Or am I just some kind of glutton for punishment?

A kid who, if he wasn't getting rocked when he was on the mound, would just sit home and whack himself over the head with a hammer?

The answer, he thought, was probably a little bit of both.

Grand Slam was the biggest indoor recreation facility

around, a huge, domed building that looked like a space-ship from the outside and had the best batting cages in the area.

A kid could spend days and days there and not get bored, since Grand Slam also offered minigolf, laser tag, bumper cars, arcade games, a tumbling room, and something called a "trampoline park."

Danny had never been on the trampolines—it was said you had to sign something like forty different forms stating you wouldn't sue if, for instance, you went flying through the air and smashed face-first through a wall and ended up sticking out the other side, like the human equivalent of a stuffed deer head.

WAIVERS ARE REQUIRED FOR ALL TRAMPOLINE PARK PARTICIPANTS read a huge sign on the door, in case anyone thought they could waltz right in.

Sammy's dad, who was a lawyer, always said the waivers "wouldn't do a darn bit of good" if a kid ever got seriously hurt. The lawsuit would be so massive, he insisted, it would close the place down.

"Letting kids play on a trampoline, that's like letting them play with a wood chipper," he'd sniff.

But Danny didn't care to find out about the dangers of bouncing around on a piece of taut fabric. When he met Mickey inside the main entrance at a little before two o'clock, he was there strictly for one purpose.

Might as well work on my hitting, he thought. The way things are going, that might be the only way I can help the team Friday—assuming Coach even lets me play some outfield after my little psycho act at the end of practice.

Mickey led him toward the back of the building where the twenty batting cages were located. Some of the other Orioles were already getting their swings in, including Sammy, Ethan, and Corey.

At the sight of Katelyn in the far cage, Danny stopped in his tracks.

"You didn't tell me the Queen of Mean was coming," Danny whispered.

"She heard about it and called me a half hour ago," Mickey said. "What was I supposed to say? 'No, you can't come, you're too annoying'? Dude, she'd probably beat me up."

"You got a point there," Danny said with a grin.

He knew Mickey was just kidding. The O's catcher was big and strong and pretty much fearless.

But no one wanted to get Katelyn mad. Because when you got her mad, her mouth started going. And when her mouth started going, the constant stream of abuse heaped your way never stopped.

You definitely wouldn't be able to concentrate on hitting with her yapping in your ear, calling you a nerd and every other name she could think of.

Danny settled into one of the cages and soon he was lost in the soothing, rhythmic sounds that surrounded him: the whirring of the pitching machines, the soft grunts of the batters as they swung, and the muted pings of balls shooting off bats.

Grand Slam had the old-fashioned "arm-style" pitching machines, which he loved. For one thing, you could see the machine's arm wind up and release the ball—almost like a real pitcher—which definitely helped the timing on your swing.

The machines were also programmed to throw no faster than sixty miles per hour, pretty much ensuring that a kid wouldn't get beaned and land in the emergency room if he failed to get out of the way of an errant pitch.

Danny was swinging so well and having so much fun that, for a while, he forgot about the Terminator deserting him and breaking his heart.

Then he heard it—a loud, gravelly voice that cut through the noise.

Judging by how quiet it got, the rest of the Orioles heard it, too.

"What do we have here? The Snore-ioles bonding over a little BP? Awww, isn't that nice!"

Whipping around, they saw it was Reuben Mendez and his Yankees posse.

They were slumped casually against the wall with their equipment bags slung over their shoulders, the harsh fluorescent lighting illuminating their navy-and-gray team T-shirts.

"It's a little late for extra hitting, isn't it?" Reuben continued, his voice lower now that he had their attention. "After all, your season ends in three days. You can take that to the bank. We plan to make sure of it."

As usual, the only one doing any talking was Reuben. The rest of the Yankees were nodding and posing and shooting the O's hard looks.

Instantly—even as he felt his palms start to sweat and his heart beat faster—Danny thought of the perfect occupation for Reuben when he grew up.

It wasn't stockbroker. Or even leg-breaker, although he definitely had a future in that, too.

No, it was movie villain.

With those beady eyes and that thick nose and cruel sneer, Danny thought, the kid would be a natural. Even now, the only thing missing when Reuben walked into a room was the ominous background music you always heard in scary movies right before the bad guy did something horrible.

And Reuben was definitely scary—as scary as any kid Danny had ever seen.

"Anyway," Reuben was saying now, "you guys should be *way* more worried about your pitching. 'Cause our lineup is gonna *rock* you Friday night."

Suddenly he pointed at Danny.

"Hey, look! It's Pizza Boy!" he said. "Heard the Terminator wasn't terminating anyone against the Indians. That's what you call it, right, the Terminator? You throw that against us, only thing that'll be terminated is you."

He folded his arms across his chest and sneered.

"Same goes for that lame starter of yours," he went on. "You know he played for us last year, right? But he didn't have that dumb name he uses now. Zip or Zoo or whatever it is."

That was enough for Katelyn.

She slammed her bat to the floor. It bounced off the hard concrete, the noise reverberating everywhere.

She took a step toward Reuben. The Orioles could see she was furious.

"The starter's name is *Zoom*, nerd," she said. "*Z-O-O-M.* You can practice it when he strikes your butt out and you're back in the dugout crying."

"Oooooh!" the other Yankees said, chuckling.

Reuben quieted them with a quick look. Then he turned back to Katelyn.

"So who are you, missy? His agent?" Reuben said. "He needs someone to stick up for him? Is that it?"

"Know who I am?" Katelyn said, eyes blazing. "I'm a fortune-teller. And I see a big oh-for-four in your future when you face us."

Danny wanted Katelyn to shut up.

He wanted to reach out and clamp a hand over her mouth in the worst way. He could see from their faces that Mickey, Sammy, and Corey felt the same way.

The way Danny saw it, as mean and unpredictable as Reuben was, he probably wouldn't smack a girl, even a nonstop taunting machine like Katelyn.

But he sure would take it out on one of the *other* Orioles if she pushed him too far.

And with my luck, Danny thought, that other Oriole will be *me*.

But getting Katelyn to stop yapping at Reuben would be tough. For one thing, she was majorly pissed off.

She was also on a roll.

"That's all you Yankees do: talk, talk, talk," she continued, flapping her fingers and thumbs together. "You think coming around here acting all big and bad scares us?"

Yes, Danny thought. Yes, it does.

"Well, it doesn't," Katelyn added. "We'll see how big and bad you are when it's game time. Now, if you'll excuse us, we've wasted enough time with you nerds."

With that, she stepped back into the batting cage, fed some coins to the machine, and resumed hitting.

Reuben and his posse seemed stunned. For a moment, they just stood there.

Finally, Reuben murmured, "Man, I'm tired of this noise" and sauntered off. The other Yankees fell in behind him, shooting dirty looks at Katelyn over their shoulders.

When they were gone, the rest of the Orioles breathed a sigh of relief. Sammy looked at Katelyn and whistled softly.

"Well," he said, "you just made Friday's game a lot more interesting."

Katelyn shrugged. "Those guys really *tick* me off," she said.

She cocked her bat, waited patiently on the next pitch, and sent a line drive screaming into the netting.

Stepping out, she locked eyes on Danny.

"You better be ready for this game, nerd," she growled. "Better be *way* better than you were the other day. Because I don't intend to lose."

26

Danny was home by himself the next morning, still shaken by Reuben's jeers and feeling major pressure from Katelyn's comments, when the doorbell rang.

Which of the usual pains-in-the-neck could this be? he wondered.

Was it the girl down the block who sold Girl Scout cookies and would always say, in a high-pitched, Chipmunks-sounding voice, "Thin mints? Tagalongs? Or how about a few boxes of our dee-licious peanut butter cookies?"

Was it the roofing contractor who seemed to show up every week and prefaced his sales pitch with "We just happen to be working in the neighborhood and wondered if you'd given any thought to putting on a new roof?"

Or was it another brochure-wielding young man in a red polo shirt and khakis trying once again to get the Connollys to switch back to cable from their current fiber-optic network?

Danny answered the door and groaned inwardly.

It was someone even more irritating than the cookie peddler, the roofing browbeater, or the cable drone.

Actually, it was two someones: Hunter and Elmo. Elmo, bent under the weight of a huge backpack stuffed to capacity, looked like a Sherpa readying to climb Mount Everest.

"Morning, D," Hunter said as the two swept past Danny and plopped themselves down in the family room.

"Why don't you guys come on in," Danny said drily, still holding the door. "Make yourselves at home."

"Sorry it took so long to get back to you," Hunter said. "Elmo was at camp all week. What was the name of the camp, E?"

"Talented Youth Physics Camp," Elmo said, brightening. "It was all about lasers and optics. We worked on using lasers for possible teleportation, quantum cryptography, quantum entanglement—"

"Whoo-hoo! Sounds like a fun time," Danny said.

"With optics," Elmo went on, "we studied the principles of reflection, refraction, diffraction, that sort of thing."

"So it was just party, party, party," Danny said.

Elmo gave him a puzzled look. He turned to Hunter for a clue, but only got a shrug.

"Anyway," Hunter said quickly, "Elmo finally got a chance to break down the videos of the Terminator and look at the measurements. Show him what you found, E."

From his backpack, Elmo withdrew a huge stack of printouts—at least three inches thick—and tossed it on the coffee table.

"What . . . is *that*?" Danny asked.

"That's the raw data collected from the videos," Elmo said. "I studied your arm action, elbow bend, release point, etc., took a number of precise measurements, and compared them to—"

"So I'm supposed to do what?" Danny interrupted, gazing at the printouts. "Take two years out of my life to go through all this? Skip my freshman and sophomore years of high school and just stay in my room, thumbing through reams and reams of data on my pitching mechanics?"

"*Or,*" Hunter said quickly, "we could have Elmo just go over the high points. You could do that, couldn't you, E?"

Elmo nodded and pulled a thin laptop from his backpack.

"It might even be better this way," he said, tapping a few keys. "I doubt either one of you could have followed the computations anyway. They're simply too complicated for most people to absorb."

Danny turned to Hunter. "He's doing it again. That condescending stuff. It makes me want to just want to grab him by the neck and push his pointy little head into a—"

"E," Hunter said nervously, "can you, um, leave out the 'I'm a genius' attitude? And just give us the results?"

"Yes, of course," Elmo said, shooting a worried glance at Danny. "Okay, when you study the two videos of when the pitch was effective and when it wasn't, you see, for instance, no difference in arm hyperabduction—"

"In English, E," Hunter said. "Not geek-speak."

"Hyperabduction," Elmo said, "has to do with getting your pitching arm above the level of your shoulders. Anyway, no difference there. The arm slot looks the same, too. So does the release point."

"Fascinating," Danny said, rolling his eyes. "So far it's been a really illuminating report."

"There *is* a slight difference in wrist angle when he snaps the ball," Elmo continued.

"So you think that's the problem?" Hunter asked.

"No, I don't," Elmo said.

He tapped a few more keys on the laptop. Another screen opened.

"And the trajectory of the pitch is a little different in the two videos," he said.

"Okay," Danny said, "so you think *that's* the problem?"

"No, I don't," Elmo said.

Danny and Hunter looked at each other.

"Okay," Hunter said. "Now I feel like murdering him myself."

"Then what *do* you think the problem is?" Danny asked.

Elmo brightened. "Oh, I *know* what the problem is. It's in the grip. Definitely in the grip."

"Okay, *now* we're getting somewhere!" Hunter said, rubbing his hands together excitedly. "Where in the grip?"

"I don't know," Elmo said, still smiling.

"You don't know," Danny repeated. "Let me get this straight. You know the problem is in the grip. But you can't tell us anything else about it?"

"Correct," Elmo said. "That's my conclusion. Based on all the metrics from the videos. With a margin of error of about, oh, two percent."

Danny and Hunter exchanged another look.

"Elmo," Hunter said in an even voice, "that's like someone going to a doctor because he doesn't feel well and being told the problem is in his back. And when the guy says, 'Where in my back?' the doctor throws up his hands and says, 'I don't know.' "

Elmo seemed to consider this for a moment.

"Regrettably, your analogy is accurate," he said. "We know—well, *I* know—the grip is the problem. Because we've eliminated all the other factors. What I don't know is if Danny is squeezing the ball too hard or holding it too lightly. Or whether he's doing something else with the grip that's interfering with the Magnus Force—"

"WARNING, WARNING: GEEK-SPEAK!" Hunter intoned in a robotic voice.

"Sorry, that's the force that results from the ball's interaction with the air," Elmo said. "The force that causes movement on a pitch. Why isn't the Terminator dropping like it used to? We don't know, because we can't get a spin-rate measurement in RPS that would effectively let us calculate—"

Danny held up his hand.

"Could you possibly—you know, for those of us who aren't world-class physicists at the age of thirteen—explain what RPS is? Thank you. Much appreciated."

Elmo nodded sheepishly.

"Revolutions per second," he said. "Bottom line: we don't know how your grip pressure is affecting how the pitch rotates and drops. Or how it *doesn't* drop, in this case."

The three of them sat in silence as Elmo's words sank in.

Finally, Danny stared at the stack of printouts and said, "You killed a lot of trees for that report. Which should probably be titled 'The Terminator: Still Not Sure Why It Sucks.' "

Hearing this, Elmo looked ready to cry.

"But look on the bright side," Hunter said. "At least we know *more* about why it sucks than we did before."

He jumped to his feet, stretched, and said, "Now that we got that out of the way, got anything to eat?"

Elmo perked up immediately.

"And would it be organic?" he asked. "Or at least vegetarian?"

A half hour later, fortified by a microwaved mushroom pizza and iced tea, Hunter and Elmo left. Danny watched them go with an empty feeling.

In forty-eight hours, the Orioles would be playing the Yankees in the biggest game of the season.

And their so-called closer—ha, like anyone would still call him a closer!—was as lost as he'd ever been in his pitching career.

Oh, Katelyn would just love to hear that.

Danny got to Eddie Murray Field early, more out of habit than any great desire to play baseball. That desire had been missing for well over a week now. Even a big game like this, with the play-offs on the line, wasn't getting him fired up.

"See you in about forty-five minutes," his mom said as she dropped him off.

Danny cocked an eyebrow. "You're coming to the game?"

"We're *all* coming," she said. "Dad doesn't have to work late. And Joey's team has a bye tonight. Isn't that great?"

Oh, yeah, Danny thought as he watched her drive away. That's just *great*. So the whole family will be on hand to watch me ride the bench. Or, if they're really lucky, they'll see me play an inning or two in left field.

It was a hot and humid Friday evening, and a half hour before game time, the stands were already filled with Yankees fans.

"Where do they *come* from?" Katelyn said as the Orioles warmed up. "The Yankees have the same amount of players as we do, right? But they always have twice as many people cheering for them. What do they do, send out invitations?"

"Maybe they recruit fans on Facebook," Sammy said. "I hear lots of teams do that now."

"That's pathetic," Katelyn said. "Why would you want strangers coming to your games? And why would the strangers *want* to come? It's not like they're giving away iPads or flat-screen TVs. Or are they?"

As the Yankees took infield, Reuben made a point of showing off on each ground ball hit to him, picking it casually on the run and throwing as hard as he could to first base. Then he glared at the Orioles as he headed back to his position.

Watching him, Katelyn couldn't help cackling.

"This kid is too much!" she cried. "Are we supposed to be impressed with that? Are we supposed to be like 'Oh, Mr. Mendez, you look fabulous taking infield! What a cannon for an arm!

"'Seeing you now, it's obvious that we don't have a chance against you and your team! What were we thinking? So we're going home now, okay? You guys win by forfeit.'"

She snorted and shook her head. "Yeah, like *that* would ever happen. Right, Zip? Or Zoo? Or whatever your dumb name is?"

"Absolutely," Zoom said. He spit a stream of sunflower seeds and shot Reuben a dirty look, punching the pocket of his glove for emphasis. "He was a jerk last year. And apparently he's still a jerk."

Zoom was totally wired for this game—the Orioles could read it on his face.

Katelyn and Sammy had filled him in earlier about Reuben's dissing of his name, as well as his trash talk about the team.

As he listened to this, Zoom's jaw had tightened and his eyes had turned into twin slits.

"Our work here is done," Katelyn had chuckled after seeing his reaction.

"Agreed," Sammy had said. "That should add at least another five miles an hour to his fastball. Especially when Reuben's up."

Danny was glad to see how loose the Orioles were, because he himself had never been more down before a game. A few minutes later, when Coach called him over, his mood only worsened.

The two of them walked down the left-field line until they were out of earshot of the team.

Danny knew what was coming. For one thing, Coach looked like his house had just burned to the ground.

"Danny," he said softly, "I've got bad news. You're not going to pitch tonight. I'll play you later in left field. But you just haven't been effective enough to pitch in a big game like this. If Zoom needs help, Sammy's going in. I'm sorry, buddy. Hope you understand."

The thing was, Danny *did* understand. But Coach's words hit him like a slap anyway.

Ever since the Terminator had gone south, he'd been pitching like crap again and everyone knew it. For the past two days, he'd tried throwing the trick pitch to Joey in the backyard and the results kept getting worse and worse.

The pitch still had zero drop, zero late movement.

It was about as hard to hit as the ocean.

But Coach had just made it official: Danny Connolly, the kid with the awesome pitch no one had ever seen before, the kid who'd been just about unhittable for weeks and the talk of the league, was back to being Gas Can Connolly.

And if the Orioles trotted him out there to face hulking Reuben Mendez and the rest of the powerful Yankees lineup, he'd only be hurting the team. That's what Coach was saying. And the last thing Danny wanted to do was hurt the team.

Walking forlornly back to the dugout, Danny noticed an old man wearing a straw hat and sunglasses leaning against the fence down the right-field line.

Mr. Spinelli had come to the game after all!

Danny waved to him and the old man waved back.

For an instant, Danny felt better. Apparently, under that grouchy demeanor, the guy actually had a heart of gold.

But Danny's spirits quickly sank again. So what if Mr. Spinelli was here? It wasn't like he was going to see a heroic pitching performance by his young next-door neighbor. All he was doing by showing up was ruining his own dinner plans—again.

And for what?

For *nothing.*

Thinking this made Danny feel even worse.

Once the game began, Zoom was uncharacteristically wild from the outset.

You didn't have to be a pitching coach to figure out why: it looked like he was trying to throw the ball 500 mph on every pitch. Everyone could see the kid was too amped up for his own good.

He walked the Yankees lead-off batter on four pitches. He walked the second kid on five pitches. Mickey jogged to the mound to calm him down. That helped for a moment as Zoom got the third batter, their lanky, power-hitting first baseman, Will Bramford, on a weak pop-up to Ethan.

It also brought Reuben strutting to the plate.

As the big shortstop dug in and took a handful of vicious practice swings, he stared balefully out at Zoom, who stared back.

"Can we move this along?" the umpire said finally. "Or do you two just want to look at each other for the whole game?"

"Yeah, let's go, Zoo," Reuben said with a smirk. "That's your name now, isn't it? We don't have all day."

Zoom's face darkened. Watching him from the dugout, Danny thought, Oh, man, this won't be good—for us or for Reuben.

Zoom rocked and kicked and threw as hard as the Orioles had ever seen him throw, a fastball that sounded like a rifle shot when it smacked Mickey's mitt.

"Ball, outside!" the ump cried.

The next pitch was another fastball out of the zone. So was the next. But rather than looking frustrated over the 3–0 count, Zoom seemed to actually be . . . *smiling*.

He reared back and fired again, and this time the pitch

just missed Reuben's chin, spinning him around and sending him sprawling in the dirt.

Reuben shot to his feet right away and dusted himself off. But the Orioles could see he wasn't smirking anymore. Or getting into another stare-off with Zoom. Trotting down to first base, he wore a look of pure relief.

Zoom kept overthrowing and walked the next batter, too, forcing in a run. Luckily for the Orioles, the next kid hit a bullet to Hunter, who doubled-up the runner on third to end the inning.

But the damage was done. The Yankees had pushed an early run across on the Orioles' best pitcher, giving them renewed confidence.

As soon as the Orioles reached the dugout, Mickey got in Zoom's face.

"Dude, you gotta calm down!" the catcher said. "Yeah, you're touching, like, three hundred miles an hour on the radar gun. But it's not helping us. Plus you're gonna kill your arm! It's gonna fall off your shoulder if you keep throwing like that!"

Zoom scowled and turned away.

"I hate those guys," he said quietly.

"Fine," Mickey said. "And I hate broccoli. But you can't let what you hate control what you do. You gotta pitch smarter than that."

Zoom shrugged and said nothing.

"ARE YOU LISTENING TO ME?" Mickey shouted, grabbing him by the jersey. "IS ANY OF THIS GETTING THROUGH?!"

Zoom looked back at his catcher, as if seeing him for the first time. His expression seemed to soften.

"Okay," he said at last, "I hear you. I'll be better next inning."

But Danny wasn't so sure, not the way Zoom was sweating and rocking nervously back and forth on the bench. The kid still had buckets of adrenaline coursing through him. Whether he could calm down enough to get his control back was anyone's guess.

The Orioles went three-up-and-three-down and Zoom was back on the mound in no time. He was still throwing hard—*way* too hard, despite both Mickey's and Coach's imploring him to slow it down.

But now the Yankees seemed so intimidated that they were swinging at anything: pitches in the dirt, pitches a foot over their heads, pitches way outside, it didn't seem to matter.

How long can he get away with that? Danny wondered.

The answer arrived quickly enough.

With the Orioles trailing 1-0 in the third inning and two out, Zoom uncorked maybe his hardest pitch of the day to Will Bramford.

Only this time the Orioles starter yelped and grabbed his arm.

Coach's face turned pale and he started immediately for the mound, but Zoom waved him off.

He kept pitching, but in visible pain now, and his fastball looked at least 10 mph slower. Only a great play by Sammy, who leaped and backhanded a scorching line drive, got the Orioles out of the inning.

As they hustled off the field, their faces were grim. It was still early and they were only down by a run. But their ace starter was grimacing in pain, cradling his arm stiffly as he walked.

Sure would be nice to have a dependable reliever besides Sammy about now, Danny thought ruefully.

On a whim, he asked Spencer to throw with him, just to see if by some miracle he could get the Terminator going again.

But he could see right away it was just as useless as before. After a half-dozen pitches, Danny threw his hands up in disgust and waved Spencer back in.

He trudged back to the dugout and sat down heavily. Feeling sorry for himself, he began flipping the ball idly from one hand to another.

The tuba, he thought, is definitely in my future.

Then he saw it.

Looking down at the ball, he noticed a small indentation next to one of the seams. Examining it more closely, he saw it was more like a tiny slash, a mark that might have been left by, say, someone's fingernail.

Danny stared at it for a few seconds. Slowly, he began to grin.

"That's it!" he whispered. "*Has* to be!"

He leaped to his feet and grabbed his glove.

Maybe someone else would think he was crazy.

Maybe someone else would think, No, it's too much of a long shot.

But Danny had never been surer of anything in his life.

"You gotta warm me up," he said to Mickey. *"Now."*

Mickey's face was pink and his hair was plastered against his forehead from the heat. He wiped himself with a towel and looked at Danny.

"Why would I do that?" he said. "You're not going in. My dad told me."

"C'mon, just a few pitches," Danny said. *"Please.* It's important."

"Right," Mickey said. "Like the fate of the entire free world rests on this."

Danny grabbed his arm. "I don't know about that," he said. "But it might help us get into the play-offs."

Mickey studied him for a moment. He sighed and reached for his face mask and mitt.

"Okay, let's go," he said. "Sure, it's ninety degrees and the humidity makes it feel like we're in a Brazilian rain forest. But there's nothing I'd rather do on a night like this than some extra bending and crouching between innings. "

They jogged out to the practice mound down the left-field line and Danny began throwing.

Seeing his first pitch, Mickey's eyes widened.

"Whoa!" he said. "Throw that again."

Danny nodded. "I had a feeling you'd say that."

He wound up and delivered again. As the ball landed in his mitt, Mickey whistled softly.

"Let's see it one more time," he said. "Just to be sure."

After Danny's third pitch, the big catcher stood and pushed up his face mask.

"It's ba-a-a-a-ck!" he sang out. "Maybe better than ever!"

Danny grinned and pumped his fist.

There was no doubt about it: the Terminator had returned—just as suddenly as it had disappeared.

Briefly, he told Mickey about the adjustment he'd just made involving the slash mark and his pinkie finger. There was no time to go into further detail, no time to say that Elmo had been right all along, so right that Danny practically felt like kissing the skinny nerd on top of his pointy little head.

As the two jogged back to the dugout, they heard a roar from the crowd. Danny looked up in time to see Corey flying around first base and heading for second as the Yankees center fielder chased down a ball in the gap.

"Oh, man, I'm up!" Mickey said, tossing his face mask aside and peeling off his shin guards. "Okay, we'll talk to my dad as soon as the inning's over."

Mickey, patient at the plate as ever, worked the count to 3–2 before hitting a sharp single to right that scored Corey with the O's first run. And Spencer kept the rally going with a run-scoring double down the right-field line.

The Yankees starter settled down after that and retired the side in order. But in the Orioles dugout, there were smiles and fist bumps all around.

They were back on top: Orioles 2, Yankees 1. The question now was: Could they hold the lead? And was Zoom too hurt to go back out there?

As soon as Coach jogged in from the third-base coach's box, Danny and Mickey ran up to him. Danny was so excited he felt light-headed.

"I can pitch if you need me," he said. "The Terminator's back. Really."

Mickey nodded. "It's totally back. Dropping better than ever, too."

"I can handle this now," Danny continued, his voice urgent. "You gotta believe me."

"It's true, Dad," Mickey said. "He's *filthy* with that pitch again."

Coach looked from one boy to another. For several seconds, he said nothing, seemingly lost in thought. He glanced over at Zoom, who groaned as he reached for his hat and glove before taking the field.

"Zoom, you're done," Coach said quietly. "Can't let you hurt that arm any more than you already have."

Zoom nodded and sat down without complaint, his arm dangling limply by his side.

"Close it out," he said to Danny. "You can *do* it."

Coach put an arm on Danny's shoulder.

"You sure you're up for this?" he asked.

"Definitely," Danny said.

"You see who's leading off for them, right?" Coach said.

Danny looked and saw Reuben Mendez lazily swinging his black bat near the on-deck circle. Even at half speed, the bat made a whistling sound as it sliced through the air.

Danny gulped. "I see him. But I'm okay."

As he jogged to the mound seconds later and began his warm-up throws, he saw the Orioles look incredulously at each other.

He knew what they were thinking: What's Coach doing? Has he lost his mind? He's bringing in Gas Can? To face the middle of the Yankees lineup?

Glancing into the stands, Danny saw his mom and dad and Joey smiling and leaning forward in anticipation. Hope I give them something to cheer about, he thought. He looked down and noticed his hands were shaking. Then it was time to focus on the game.

When Reuben dug in, the Orioles could see the big shortstop's smirk was back. Bigger and bolder than ever. Like it had never left.

Easy to see why, Danny thought. Reuben had to be thrilled to see that another Zoom fastball wouldn't be crackling under his chin. He was probably just as thrilled that—based on recent reports—he was facing a junk-ball pitcher missing a key ingredient: a junk ball that could actually get someone out.

"Bring it, Pizza Boy!" he sang out, earning a look from the ump.

Danny took a deep breath, checked his grip, rocked, and fired.

The pitch sailed to the plate in all its limp, humpbacked, wet-diaper glory. Reuben's eyes lit up and his front leg began to stride forward. Just as he began to uncoil, the pitch seemed to stop and hover in place before plummeting to earth.

Reuben's swing caught nothing but air.

The umpire's right hand shot up.

"Stee-rike!"

Danny was so relieved to see the Terminator working again that he almost broke out in giggles.

Now the Yankees shortstop stepped out, muttering to himself. He fiddled with his batting gloves, glaring the whole time at Danny, and stepped back in.

Mickey put down the sign for the rainmaker version of the Terminator.

Perfect, Danny thought. Hadn't Mr. Spinelli talked about mixing up his pitches? Maybe Danny wasn't following the old man's advice to the letter. But at least he was mixing up his Terminators now.

He floated this one a good two feet higher than the previous one. Reuben craned his neck and gazed skyward. Danny could see the uncertainty on his face, could see him jerking the bat off his shoulder, wondering whether to swing.

Ultimately he decided not to. The ball landed in Mickey's mitt with a soft *WHUMP!*

"Stee-rike two!" said the ump.

Reuben whipped around and snarled, "Are you serious?!"

The ump jerked off his mask.

"Play ball, son," he growled. "You're really starting to push it." Then, to the Yankees dugout, he said, "That's a warning."

Go ahead, kid, Danny thought. *Keep arguing.* In eight years of playing ball, he had yet to see a single instance when mouthing off to an ump did any good for a batter, or helped a team in any way.

Usually it was just the opposite: now the ump was looking for any excuse to ring you up. The pitch could be six inches off the plate and he'd call it a strike.

The smirk was gone again from Reuben's face, replaced by a look of cold anger.

He kicked furiously at the dirt and stepped in again, holding his bat high and waving it in menacing little circles.

Danny nodded as Mickey signaled for the exact same pitch. When it shot into the sky, Reuben started his swing. To his horror, the ball hung there, as if floating from a tiny parachute. When the pitch finally began its descent, he jerked the bat back and tried to swing again.

A double swing!

Danny had never seen anything like it. Reuben missed it by two feet. The follow-through was so ferocious that he twisted his legs in a knot and collapsed awkwardly in a heap.

"Stee-rike three!"

From the stands came the sounds of muffled laughter. Even in the Yankees dugout, players could be seen hiding their faces behind their gloves as they cracked up.

Reuben leaped to his feet and pointed at Danny.

"You're so freaking lucky!" he shouted. "The game's not over, boy. I'll get you next time."

Danny breathed a sigh of relief. He looked down at his hands.

They weren't shaking anymore.

Danny knew this was the time to take Mr. Spinelli's advice.

This was the perfect moment, after getting past the Yankees' fearsome slugger, to start mixing up his pitches and keep the rest of the team's hitters off-balance.

But he didn't.

The Terminator had done so well paralyzing one of the best hitters in the league that Danny just kept throwing it.

He struck out the next kid on three pitches. The next Yankees batter resorted to the usual desperation measure of sticking out his arm to let the pitch graze it.

Coach bolted from the dugout and protested—in vain, it turned out—that the kid had made no effort to get out of the way. But Danny quickly struck out the next batter on three straight Terminators to end the inning.

Jogging off the mound, he could see the Yankees talking about the pitch and exchanging confused looks.

Their coach kept yelling at everyone to relax, which

Danny knew was the first clue of a panicked team. How could you relax when your coach was running around like his hair was on fire?

To make things even more chaotic, Reuben had picked up a bat and appeared to be giving some of the Yankees an impromptu lesson on how to attack the Terminator, all while the ump was shouting at them to take the field.

Beautiful, Danny thought.

The kid looks absolutely lost on three straight swings and now he's an expert on how to hit the thing.

As soon as the Orioles were back in the dugout, Katelyn marched up to him.

"Nerd, what *is* it with you?" she demanded. "One week you suck, then you're great, then you suck again. And now you're back to looking All-Universe. With a pitch that looks like something a mad baseball scientist dreamed up in a lab somewhere."

"That's me: Mr. Consistency," Danny said. "Part of my charm."

"Just don't go back to being Mr. No Clue," Katelyn said. "Keep focusing, nerd. The game's not over yet."

"Like that's a news flash," Mickey muttered as she went off to get a drink. Then, in a deep announcer's voice, he intoned, "This just in: a regulation baseball game for the thirteen-and-under age group consists of six innings! Now back to our regular programming."

Danny laughed. Here they were, playing in the biggest game of the season, and the big catcher was still cracking jokes and trying to keep his pitcher loose.

Danny wasn't exactly loose—he knew the Terminator could again disappear just as suddenly as it returned, all because of some tiny flaw in his grip or delivery or whatever. But he was feeling a lot better about the pitch than he had earlier in the day.

The Orioles went down in order and Danny was back on the mound in the fifth inning with little rest. But if anything, the Terminator looked even more effective against the Yankees' eight, nine, and one hitters.

After Danny struck out the first kid on a towering Terminator, the Orioles could hear the Yankees coach yelling to his team, "You gotta be patient up there! Wait for your pitch!"

But when the second kid struck out on a similar pitch, the coach, a big swaggering man wearing dark sunglasses, shouted, "You gotta be more aggressive and attack that pitch!"

This is hilarious, Danny thought, trying hard not to smile. Like something you'd see on Comedy Central, only maybe funnier.

When the third batter went down swinging to end the inning, Danny half expected the Yankees coach to say, "C'mon! You gotta be patiently aggressive up there!"

Instead, the coach simply shook his head in disgust and muttered, "You're making this guy look like an all-star out there!"

When the Orioles came off the field, Coach took Danny aside.

"How do you feel?" he asked. "Look, you've been great. But if you're getting tired, I can have Sammy warm up."

Danny looked at him as if he'd lost his mind.

Leave the game now? With just one inning to go? Leave a situation where he was finally helping the team after the up-and-down—okay, mostly down—season he'd had?

Not a chance.

But all he said was "I'm good, Coach. Really."

Coach glanced at his scorebook. "Their two, three, and four hitters are up next inning," he said. "Which means you'll be facing your buddy Reuben again."

Danny nodded grimly. "I know."

Only this time, he thought, we'll have a little surprise in store for Mr. Mendez.

The Orioles were still clinging to a 2–1 lead when they took the field in the top of the sixth inning, the noise level rising all around them.

Danny was surprised that he was feeling nervous again. He struck out the first batter on four pitches, which brought Will Bramford to the plate.

In many ways, Will scared Danny even more than Reuben did, because he was such a disciplined hitter. Whereas Reuben was a free-swinging behemoth who could turn a checked swing into a home run, the scouting report on Will was that he rarely swung at anything out of the strike zone—and when he swung, he connected.

Danny knew the Terminator would have to work perfectly to get Will. With his heart hammering in his chest, he threw three of the best he had thrown all season, with Will taking his smooth, level swing at all three and missing each by a foot.

The Yankees were down to their last out.

Danny took a deep breath.

Under his breath, he uttered in a PA announcer's voice, "Now batting for the Evil Empire: Reuben Mendez."

With both the Orioles and Yankees fans on their feet, Danny signaled for Mickey to join him for a conference. Briefly, he explained how he wanted to pitch Reuben.

"Perfect," Mickey said with a grin. "Diabolical. Almost bordering on evil. But . . . perfect. I'm impressed."

Danny shook his head.

"Before you get too impressed," he said, "let's see if it actually works."

As Reuben strutted to the plate, Danny rubbed up the ball and looked around the little ballpark.

How cool is this? he thought. Two outs, me facing their best hitter with the game on the line. If we win, we go to the play-offs. If we lose, well, I'll probably be playing way too much Spider-Man from now on.

The whole scene felt like something out of one of those sports movies he loved so much. Except he knew that in real life, major league closers dealt with this kind of pressure every day during the season.

"Time to be a real closer right here," he murmured to himself.

Seeing Reuben dig in, Danny nearly gasped. The kid had completely changed his batting stance. His right leg was now bent at almost a ninety-degree angle and his entire torso was tilted back, so that his chin, left elbow, and shoulders pointed to the sky.

Like he thought the Terminator would be dropping directly overhead from a helicopter or something.

It was almost comical to see. No, it *was* comical, Danny decided. Except he was way too tense to laugh.

He looked at the sign from Mickey, which was really a fake sign, since they both knew what was coming.

He went into his windup, rocked, kicked, and delivered. Reuben was still looking up, waiting for the Terminator to do its high, slow tumble toward him.

What he got was a fastball on the inside corner for strike one.

Clearly shocked, he stepped out and scowled at Danny.

"What, you don't want to throw that junk again?" he shouted. "Afraid I'll rock you this time?"

Danny ignored him. This was no time to get into a trash-talking contest. He needed to concentrate. The big shortstop could still tie the game with one swing of the bat if Danny wasn't careful.

Reuben dug in again and dropped into the same goofy stance, chin and upper body pointed even higher now.

He gritted his teeth and tilted back so far he seemed in danger of tipping over.

Danny got the sign, wound up, and fired.

Again Reuben stood there looking bewildered, the bat never leaving his shoulder as a sharp curve ball broke across his thighs.

Strike two.

Now he was more agitated than ever. He stepped out and took a couple of vicious practice swings, muttering to himself and staring at Danny the whole time.

When he stepped back in, he was still leaning back like a palm tree in a hurricane.

"Throw it!" he shouted. "Why won't you throw it?"

Danny shook his head in amazement. It was like his dad always said: some people never learn. This was a textbook example.

Going into his windup, he thought, *Okay, see what you can do with this.*

As soon as the pitch was on its way, Reuben's eyes widened with confusion. Frantically, he tried to level his hips and bring his arms down to get the bat moving.

Too late—*way* too late—his brain processed what it was that was coming his way: another fastball.

It split the middle of the plate.

Strike three.

Reuben flung his bat in disgust and slammed his helmet in the dirt.

For Danny, what happened next was all a blur.

He stole a quick glance at the stands and saw his mom and dad and Joey jumping up and down, hugging each other and laughing. He turned and saw Mr. Spinelli down the right-field line, cheering and waving his hat in the air.

In the next instant, he was engulfed by the rest of the Orioles, lost at the bottom of a happy pig pile that seemed to last forever.

Danny regarded the painting thoughtfully for several moments and finally threw up his hands.

"Okay, I give up," he said. "What's it supposed to be? Is it some sort of a garden? Or just, like, a lot of colors splashed together to look cool?"

Mr. Spinelli spluttered with indignation.

"Are you *serious*?" he began. "Because if you are, you need to go have your eyes checked, boy. Have them check your brain, too, while they're at it."

Danny shrugged. "Is it a beach scene? Wow, if that's it, it's not a great beach. The colors are all wrong. And where are the waves? And the seagulls? Maybe you just weren't feeling it that day. Just sayin' . . ."

The old man walked over to where the painting hung on one wall. He jabbed a bony finger at it and shot a murderous look back at Danny.

"You can't see that this is Eddie Murray Field?" he asked. "And that here's the diamond and the trees ringing the outfield and the bleachers? And that this is the big, brick concession stand?"

"Ohhhh," Danny said, still playing dumb. "A *concession* stand. I thought that was like a giant red frog or something."

"A giant red frog?!" Mr. Spinelli repeated. "Son, what has happened to you? Did you get hit in the head when you played the Yankees? Is that the problem? Because I'm not sure I've ever met anyone as dense as you in my entire life."

Finally, Danny could hold it in no longer. He burst out laughing, pointed at the old man, and said, "Gotcha!"

Mr. Spinelli shook his head and gave a sigh of relief.

"Okay, you definitely had me going," he said. "Anyone ever tell you that you have a sick sense of humor?"

"Only my mom and dad and Joey," Danny said. "And all my teachers and friends. And anyone who's ever known me for more than five minutes."

"Well, they're all right," Mr. Spinelli muttered. "Talk about almost giving an old guy a near heart attack. . . ."

"Sorry," Danny said, turning back to the painting. "The truth is, this is wonderful, Mr. S. Can't thank you enough for the great gift."

It was a week later, and even though the Orioles' season was over, thanks to a first-round play-off loss to the Twins, Danny was in a fine mood.

Despite the fact that he and Zoom had pitched well—the Terminator, in fact, had continued to be the talk of the league—the Orioles bats had gone into a bit of a slump at the worst possible time.

Still, as Coach had pointed out, the O's had nothing to be ashamed of and a lot to look forward to for next season.

Moments earlier, Danny had been walking past Mr. Spinelli's house when the old man had stuck his head out the second-floor window and shouted, "Boy, come up here! I've got something for you."

Now here he was in Mr. Spinelli's art studio, admiring the new painting and talking baseball with his elderly neighbor, who seemed way less grouchy than he did before.

"So you figured out what was wrong with your new pitch, eh?" the old man said as he rinsed off some brushes in the sink.

Danny nodded. "It was so weird. I saw this slash mark on the ball, right? Turns out I was digging my pinkie fingernail into the cover right before I let it go. Which means I was squeezing it *way* too hard."

"Yep," Mr. Spinelli said, "that's all it takes to throw the pitch off. You have to hold it like you'd hold an egg. And throw it that way, too. Otherwise, it just won't behave the way you want it to."

"Anyway, Elmo was right," Danny said. "I can't believe it, but it's true. He said the problem was with the grip."

Mr. Spinelli looked puzzled. "Elmo?"

"This nerdy kid I know," Danny said. "He's a physics whiz. He tried to help me figure out what was wrong. I was pretty mean to him. But in the end, he knew what he was talking about."

"God save us from the baseball nerds and the sabermetrics crowd," Mr. Spinelli said with a chuckle.

"The *what* crowd?" Danny asked.

"Sabermetrics," the old man repeated. "It's the mathematical and statistical analysis of the game. Over-the-top, if you ask me. They want to turn it into this soulless, numbers-crunching exercise."

"Sounds pretty boring," Danny said. "Think I'd rather play it."

Actually, Danny had been thinking a lot about his baseball future over the last several days.

The Terminator, he realized, was a special pitch that had made the game fun for him again after his crappy start. Just as importantly, it had helped his parents realize there was more than one ballplayer in the family who deserved some attention.

And now that he'd learned the checkpoints of what to look for when the Terminator wasn't working so well, Danny was sure he'd be more consistent with it, too. And more patient with it. As Joey said, sometimes you just had to wait for things to work themselves out.

But Danny also planned to take Mr. Spinelli's advice to start mixing up his pitches. Heck, that—and the element of surprise—had worked against a certain bad-tempered Yankees slugger, hadn't it? Which meant Danny needed to do some serious work to upgrade his fastball, curve, and changeup over the off-season.

Besides, he thought, marching around in the hot sun with a tuba looked like way too much work. You practically had to be a weight lifter to lift the stupid thing, never mind lug it all over the field at halftime of a high school football game.

As the old man dried his paintbrushes, Danny said, "Can I ask you a question?"

Mr. Spinelli shrugged. "Even if I said no, you wouldn't listen to me. So go ahead, ask away."

"You told me one reason you quit playing ball was because you were a perfectionist," Danny said. "You couldn't control that junk pitch all the time and you got frustrated. But what was the other reason?"

The old man took off his glasses and rubbed his eyes wearily. "Here we go again. Another interrogation by Detective Danny Connolly."

"Sorry," Danny said. "If you don't want to tell me . . ."

"No, it's okay," Mr. Spinelli said. "If you must know, I fell in love. Madly, deliriously, passionately in love. The girl was in college in another state. Suddenly baseball wasn't the most important thing in my life. So I moved to be with her."

He stared out the window and sighed.

"*That* I never regretted for a moment," he went on. "We were married fifty years. She died just before we were supposed to move in here. The place is kind of empty without her."

A moment later, he seemed to cheer up. "But I can't complain. We had a great life together. And now that you and I are buddies—unless you get too annoying—maybe you'll come over every once in a while to keep me company."

"That would be awesome," Danny said. "Maybe we could even talk about your college baseball career."

The old man's eyes twinkled. "Baseball's a waste of time—didn't somebody tell you that? But, yeah, maybe we can talk about that, too."

With that, he handed Danny the painting of Eddie Murray Field and said, "All right, you better get going. I have some work to do."

Danny turned to leave and suddenly stopped.

"I have a favor to ask," he said. "Think you could teach me how to paint?"

Mr. Spinelli cocked an eyebrow. "You? I had no idea you were interested in art."

"Oh, I am," Danny said. He pointed at another painting. "For instance, I'd love to be able to paint something like that brown rug."

The old man's eyes narrowed.

"Let me get this straight," he said. "You think that's a *rug*?"

"Sure," Danny said. "Isn't it?"

Mr. Spinelli stared at him.

"For your information," he said, "that's a painting of a vintage baseball glove, circa 1925. Just like the one Babe Ruth used."

Danny studied it again.

"Oh," he said. "My bad."

Then he cracked up and pointed at Mr. Spinelli. "Gotcha again!" he cried. "You're too easy!"

The old man smiled and shook his head.

"You're killing me, kid," he said. "Absolutely killing me."